# FISHING IN BEIRUT

Steven Callaghan

BLUE PRESS

ISBN 978-0-9565960-0-0

Cover design by Shrinking Velvet Designs
Cover copyright © Shrinking Velvet Designs 2010
www.shrinkingvelvet.com

A CIP catalogue record of this book is available from the British Library
Printed & bound in Great Britain by Lightning Source UK Ltd.,
Milton Keynes.

# FISHING IN BEIRUT

*We walk on*
*an unsilvered*
*mirror,*
*a crystal surface*
*without clouds.*
*If lilies would grow*
*backwards,*
*if roses would grow*
*backwards,*
*if all those roots*
*could see the stars*
*and the dead not close*
*their eyes,*
*we would become like swans.*

*- Federico Garcia Lorca*

*There's someone dying on the balcony above. They're coughing and coughing, and it doesn't sound good. An ominous death rattle. It blends with the music in Frank's room, making it sound even harsher. It starts and stops, and there is silence, and then suddenly a volley of phlegm-flavoured drum roll crackles in the dusk, and ripples out to mix with occasional traffic, birdcalls, and Frank's music. Frank's music from the flat below.*

*Frank is twenty three, and lives in Paris. He sits in his room, plays solitaire with a three-card turnover. His hair is too long, but he has no friends here who will cut it. He doesn't want to go to a hairdresser.*

*Many people have cut Frank's hair. Some are no longer friends, and some are, and live in Berlin, and Chicago, and Sevilla, and elsewhere. Dublin too, where Frank was born.*

*The coughing won't stick to a pattern. It starts and stops, and there is silence, and then suddenly...The interval is never the same. It's the sound of an ailing body Frank is hearing. A sharp and frightening cough, braying for all the sick and lonely of the world.*

*It's not dark yet, but the sun is slipping. The birds move toward their homes in military formations. Traffic occasionally, but less than before. Frank's music is making him cry. He wants to hear the air, the space, the distant freeway motion, not this wretched coughing, and no longer this oily tune. He turns it off abruptly, and there's nothing on the street below. The coughing's gone, and that's a faraway carhorn. It's peaceful and small, and oddly too it's warm – strangers going home in cars he doesn't know. He moves to his window and wipes his trickling cheeks, and leans out, solitary, in the cool evening calm. And then there is the cough.*

*He pushes back in disgust. Slams the window, but feels too hot and stuffy. Opens it again, resigning himself to this raucous torture. A bronchial hacking, slashing at his ears.*
*Frank's trousers are torn in several places. Random holes here and there. His shirt is creased and open.*
*"Open up your shirt honey," a girl had said once, with laughter, and gentle calming mockery.*

5

*A distant, distant time, a half-forgotten place.*
*"Open up your shirt, and let me touch your skin."*

*An Italian girl in a German city, who said shirts opened up, and*
*performance opened out. "Open up your shirt," and Frank had*
*complied.*

*He walks around the room in a circle, making it bigger,*
*smaller, on each tiny lap. He paces about, and God's sky*
*darkens.*

*Buttons coming free, his breathing growing rapid.*
*"Open up your shirt Frankie, open up your shirt."*

\*

*The coughing has abated, the day is fully night. Frank's cigarette*
*glows brightly, and you won't find a light on here. Breathing*
*growing rapid, in a distant, distant place.*

# GETTING THERE

And so that's a blind girl at the bus stop. It's windy, busy on the street, and the bus comes along and she doesn't put out her hand, and the bus doesn't stop, and her name is Karen. It's rue de Vaugirard, outside Jardin du Luxembourg, at three o'clock in the afternoon. Her brown hair is blown and whipped, but she has only been told it's brown, and to her that doesn't mean a thing.

Karen thinks she hears the bus engine approach and puts out her hand. But it's a truck, and it's busy on the street, and it does not stop, because it's a truck. She is confused and thinks the bus is passing, and calls out stop, holding aloft her white stick. She doesn't know what's happening, and people must be looking now. She pushes back her hair, and moves to the wall.

She sighs and coughs, annoyed that bus didn't stop. Now her boyfriend will be waiting, and he'll grow anxious, and she'll grow anxious on his behalf. Everyone tells her to buy a cell phone. Probably she should. She's twenty-six, and they tell her she's beautiful. They told her in Chicago, and everyone tells her here.Michel is beautiful. She knows that for sure. The way he feels, the way his breath feels, the way it quickens when they... the way it's not his skin that's warm, more his body underneath. He's waiting for her now she knows, north of the river, and he's probably getting worried. She exhales slowly, her shoulders rising and falling.

Someone else has arrived beside her. There is the rustle of a jacket, a face being scratched, male, and almost imperceptible breathing. Suddenly a heavy intake and exhalation, nasally, which sounds like a thunderclap as she listens carefully.

The man coughs, sniffs, scratches his face again. A man with an affliction, an affliction or a prop, born of sinuses, or habit, or tar settled snugly on the lungs. A faint and commonplace prelude of death, and a nag to go along with his having to wait for a bus. Karen rubbed her hands and waited silently. Wednesday.

Frank sat by the river and smoked grass. The October sun made flashes on the water, disturbed only by passing sightseeing cruisers. He spat off the *quai*, shivered in his filthy jacket, and eyed forlornly a small girl waving from a boat. She smiled with dancing eyes, but he didn't lift his hand.

*'Andamos*
*sobre un espejo*
*sin azogue,*
*sobre un cristal*
*sin nubes.*
*Si los lirios nacieran*
*al reves,*
*si las rosas nacieran*
*al reves,*
*si todas las raices*
*miraran las estrellas*
*y el muerto no cerrara*
*sus ojos,*
*seriamos como cisnes.'*

Frank knew this poem off by heart, but he didn't know what it meant. Never picked up Spanish in Sevilla, never had the inclination to. He saw this lack of knowledge as being unimportant, because the act of recitation bore its own weight for him. He rubbed an insect bite on his hand, and by doing so set in train a constant need to do so. Gratification only came when he stopped.

There was a smell of urine from the bank below. He shifted about, his jeans scraping stone. The night before he had been out walking late,and had looked up and seen a man in a window, like a distant yellow tv screen, talking on a phone. Silhouetted dreadlocks, and the warm African French carried down softly on the chill wind.

"Non, mais dis-moi," the man had murmured. "Je ne peux pas attendre."

If he could get up to that room, and go down that phoneline, and wind up next to the other speaker, what world would he have entered? A bedroom or a kitchen, a bathroom or a hall? Maybe he'd be in an alley, on a street, and what is it that's needed, and what just cannot wait? And what if after that call someone called the caller, this man who is somewhere else, and he went down *that* phoneline, and on and on. Would he end up beside someone he knew? Would he have passed by needles and agony to get from here to there? Have spied on naked skin, heard yelping dogs?

Frank had let his mind wander and thrown away his beercan, and wound up nowhere but home, alone and out of drink. Now a day later he sits by the Seine, and he won't even wave to a child from who knows where, a child who when she's fifty will say once I was in Paris.

He rolled his neck and spat. Slick saliva puddle kissing pissy Paris ground. He lay down on his back and there were no clouds overhead. Concrete coldness seeped through the hair on his head, permeating the back of his skull, hurting the bones. He sat back up and re-attacked the insect bite. It gave as good as it got.

There was a flutter to the left, and he turned to see a pigeon strutting about like one of those rappers talking ice and bitches, head and shoulders in motions of brain dead arrogance. He raised his arm violently, and it hopped and cooed and flew. There was near stillness by the water now.
Ripples.

Frank got up and pissed by the *quai* wall. Two American tourists marched by, the woman clucking in disdain. The swish of anoraks and jeans. He watched them powerwalk over the cobbles, gesturing as they spoke.

They grew smaller, too distant to be heard. Then they disappeared around the bend.

Johnny gets up, and God only knows what her name in that bed is, but he is out the door, with laces not yet tied. It's seven or eight, an early workday morning, and the air is doing that tickling thing that makes him want to shake with joy. He turns up his collar and nearly trips over his laces.

Further down the street, which is called Alesia, he stops and ties them. Stops and ties them, looks like kneeling in a pew. Whatshername had clamped her leg over him when they finished, and left it there, grip-like, till morn. Between his shoulder blades throbbed slowly from the wriggling movements necessary to get free.

Whatshername was the latest in a long line of whatshernames. She had kissed like she was thirsty. If he closed his eyes now on rue d'Alesia he could still be back in her room, looking down upon her in her cramped orange bed, her face blurring, the smell of her skin.

Johnny was thirty two, sometimes said thirty, and others thirty five. Sometimes mumbled thirty three, *"like Jesus."* The temporary Christ of the lonely single business girl, the ragged fucking Saviour, who rolled his own stone from the mouth of the cave come earthly break of day.

Every day for the past two years he had sat in front of the Centre Georges Pompidou and played acoustic guitar – not for money, not for the benefit of the tourists. How he fed and clothed himself was a mystery even to him, or at least was a mystery when he forgot about selling coke. He forgot as often as he could.

He arrived from Senegal three years before, known to all there as Jean, intimidated initially by choked Parisian sprawl. A room in the Goutte d'Or and the phone number of a distant cousin in case things got rough. He'd never called this cousin. Jean did become Johnny, and acquired a full-length leather coat, and lived predominantly on crisps and dry baguette, and cheap domestic champagne. He spoke English to Pompidou sightseers in a good mood, and scowled endlessly at nothing at all in a bad one.

He sat there all day, was visited by many, and occasionally went entire weeks without playing so much as a note.

The darkness brought a hunger, and living things will feed. At night he walked into bars in potent places, and he knew the type he was looking for. The stylish attire, the make-up, but the bouncing of the dainty shoe on the foot and the demure dart-away glance betraying an at-heart office girl fed up competing with the boys. Where was her romance? her wistful lipcurl wondered, her mystery enigma – her knight in battered leather, whose breathing made hers fast. Well there he was across the floor, and he was looking at you. He would wake up in the morning to another commentellesappelle.

He stopped into a bakery on rue d'Alesia and emerged a minute later with pain au chocolat. Stuffed the wrapping into a pocket and devoured. He didn't think he'd ever been here before, but a sign said Denfert Rochereau up ahead, and that was on Ligne 4, and Ligne 4 went to Chateau Rouge, which was the closest stop to Johnny's room on crumbling rue Leon. He could return and get the guitar, and be back at Beaubourg before today had even started.

Karen woke up to the radio. Tuesday. She lay in bed for ten minutes, until it told her it was quarter to ten. She got up and showered.

Breakfast was always muesli and fruit juice, because they all agreed this is a good combination to begin a new day. All those voices on television health shows.

Karen's tv was essentially a bigger, bulkier radio. She often wondered what country had made it, and why the hell she'd taken it when the man upstairs had died and it was destined for the trash. Poor old Monsieur Boulier, who had always been polite.

She listened to it while ironing, or dusting around the flat. It told her many things, and plunged her aurally into hackneyed adventures. When it spoke of healthy eating she listened carefully.

She finished off the muesli and washed the bowl. Started the machine for coffee. It popped away noisily. She was wearing the shirt that scratched her wrists while she was reading, which was always second to last on the left side of the shirts and blouses closet. It was next to the one she never wore now.

She went to the fridge and got more juice. Did some ironing. The warm feeling of the fabric where the iron had just been, in comparison with the rest. Birds chattered through the open window, some near some far. She leaned her head out and felt the sun.

The ironing got done, and so the board went back into the tiny space between the kitchen table and the wall. It slouched against the wall in relief, free from scalding till the next time. Karen carried the clothes to her bed – she dropped and then sorted.

On the phone she spoke to her mother, asked after life in leafy Oak Park. Got another call, switched to it, mumbled morning sweetness's to Michel in French, and switched back to Mom. Dorothy had just adopted an Iraqi baby, who was to be called Georgie. Dorothy was Mom's best friend, and at the age of 58 had left her husband Archie, and struck out on her own.

Dorothy was Mom's shining light. She gave hope, while Karen was in France. She had apparently joked about how the Iraqi baby did not need clothes, because with all the international red tape he had been carried through some had inevitably stuck, and little Iraqi Georgie was now guaranteed warmth for life. Mom thought this was just so funny. Karen laughed a little too. "So are there any plans to come home honey?" she was asked. "No, I don't think so – I still really like it here." "And how is the boyfriend?" "Michel." "Yes the boyfriend. How is he?" "He's fine Mom," said Karen. "He's fine and says hello."

Later that night, she lay awake and listened to footsteps up above. The not-so-new new tenant. Old Monsieur Boulier's face had felt like an ancient raincoat.

When Frank left, Berlin had put one thought in his head: freedom soars over all. Then came Chicago, came Sevilla, and f reedom started drifting. If he craned around his neck, and stared back into the past, the bus out of Berlin was when the bubble burst.

The soup stain on his trousers is not going away. He feels it looks unsightly as he walks down rue de Rennes, this chill December weekend. There are girls with dainty black gloves and precision perfect make-up. There are grown men who act like boys, and some of them with dainty black gloves also. Stylish beige attire abounds, saliva lips of shoppers like aroused blood dogs. Frank is uncomfortable in this. He reaches Montparnasse and collapses to the ground. He hasn't eaten in two days, because he wanted to test his strength. He gurgles and spits, and there's a tingling in the limbs. It's warm, fuzzy – tiny internal dots of rhythmical motion. Frank is on the ground beside a congealed chewing gum.

A security guard from a lingerie boutique helps him up. He is fixing his collar for him when Frank sags. He is only standing now because of this man.

All around there are people. All around, too much is going on. Voices from everywhere, with a sharpness to the afternoon air. Frank is assisted to a bench by his benefactor. Wood meets bone and tissue as he slumps. The man is asking after his present awareness, but Frank can't remember the French he knows. His whole face is lolling.

# ARIA

The airport in San Jose is called Mineta. She sits there waiting, her hand luggage on the seat beside her, the rest already checked in. She keeps bouncing her foot, because that's what waiting is all about. It's a daytime flight to New York, then an overnight to Paris. There is waiting before take-off, and waiting between flights.

The humming artificiality of airports affects people unknowingly. There is stress in travel preparations, stress in morning crowds, in electric lighting when it's clear and blue outside. In baggage, queues, insanely loud gum chewing.

But there is beauty too. Aria is more excited than nervous, and she no longer gets stressed so easily. When she sits near the enormous windows she can see the planes taking off and landing, and the tiny men in orange jackets somehow directing the chaos. She can see birds, sun, and the endless expanse of runway. She can see her city's buildings, a distant glinting skyline.

She can find calm within the hum, and embrace how she feels right now, sitting on this chair. She can see herself at five, splashing in the ocean, and on this airport chair feel that tingling in her legs.

On the plane the stewardess pointed out the exits. "In case of emergency, inflate the lifejacket by pulling firmly on the cord." Aria listened attentively. A man two rows in front stood up too quickly and whacked his head off the air conditioner knob. "Jesus Christ," he muttered, and the stewardess bade him be seated.

She sleeps and wakes up in New York. Missed the aerial descent, missed the glaring absence of the Twin Towers on the Manhattan skyline. Someone's laboured breathing as he fishes a bag from the compartment above her head wakes her upon landing. He gets hers while he's up there, handing it to her carefully, and they all file off together.
"I do not know *what* to make of this place," he tells her as they shuffle up the tunnel, sounding like a cowboy.

There was a five-hour wait for the Paris connection. She spent it by the window. Once she turned around and spied the cowboy, way over the other side of the terminal, sitting down eating a sandwich, until he was eclipsed by six Asian women, all wearing matching white jumpers. It grew dusk, and then dark. There was so much talking among the throng of people it almost seemed like there was silence. People swirled around, telling jokes, reporting to companions on boarding time updates, looking nervously about for toilets. Night-time now, and she felt she might be too tired to sleep on this final journey. Crestfallen momentarily, she suddenly looked up happily, and remembered she was going to Paris.

There was minor turbulence halfway through the flight. It woke her as the dawn broke. It was untroubling to most, but one woman began hyperventilating. Rapid gasping could be heard towards the front, as her body dragged in extra air. A paper bag and a soothing touch helped restore the imbalance.

Aria officially turned nineteen ten minutes after. February 6th. She placed her hand on her abdomen to feel the gentle rising and falling, and smiled. So this was her nineteenth birthday. Clouds formed God-like formations out the left-hand window – heartpiercing endless death white, crystal heaven sun stabs. It was nearly too much to look at. The aching destined blue of the uninterrupted sky, stretching out unending till the rational explodes. The space, and the calming airplane breath hum, that sent her half to sleep.

She read the in-flight magazine, and drank some water. Time passed. Somewhere someone coughed, amidst the low scattered chatter and the intermittent toilet traffic. There was an article on Berlin, "Europe's City Of Wild." It said the whole city centre had been undergoing rebuilding for some time, around Potsdamer Platz. She looked at a picture of a crane filled skyline, and thought it beautiful.

Flicking through the magazine, she was hit with credit card advertisements, fold-out perfume samples, a black and white photograph of Vienna. She returned to the Berlin article.

The writer mentioned an abundance of drug use in Berlin. He attempted to speak knowingly of this for a paragraph, but then returned to detailing tourist attractions. The Memorial Church, the TV Tower at Alexanderplatz, built to facilitate spying on the West over the wall. The Brandenburg Gate. She looked at little pictures of these, all backed by a sky that seemed too poetically pink streaked. She got up and walked the length of the aircraft slowly, because what is that blood disease airplanes give you now.

Later more drinks were brought, and she had orange juice. Her legs were restless and tired all at once. She could see the ocean down below, minute seagulls darting, sea-spray. The radio on the armrest had a station playing reggae, but only her left headphone was working. She was getting mostly bass at the expense of treble, and the system was fuzzing under the strain.

Paris was growing nearer. A snake of excitement wriggled in her back, liquid-like, momentarily. She sensed into her body on the seat. A baby started crying, but then changed its mind and laughed. It gurgled and cooed, and Aria couldn't help smiling.

Someone started using a discman, and a stewardess ran frantically down the aisle in search of the culprit. Upon discovery, she issued the hapless baggy-jeaned teen a lecture on the dire effect it could have on the cockpit controls. He flicked his fringe out of his eyes and stared at her open-mouthed. Her cheeks swelled puffer fish-like as she rebuked him. His knee started jumping, and it grew harder to feign nonchalance. The stewardess noticed this, upped the tempo of her tirade, and Aria felt sorry for the guy. She tried to smile at him when the woman left, but his eyes were boring holes into the seat in front, his body rigid.

And so the flight ended. The plane touched down, all shudders bumps and hiss, and Charles de Gaulle flicked by as they taxied. Sun shining. She stayed seated till the fasten seat belt sign had been switched off, was careful when opening the overhead compartment, lest any luggage had been dislodged. A sunlight laser shot through a far window, illuminating dust rising off the seats.

It occurred to her that this much dust was everywhere, whether it could be seen or not, and she tried to breathe less. Her bag strap felt slippy in her slight palm sweat. She readjusted her grip.

Queues, passports, conveyor belts of other peoples possessions, and hers somewhere in among them. She saw her own swinging around, and dragged it off onto one of those euro deposit trolleys. This euro was what they all used in Europe now. It was a strange little thing. She felt it jangling in her jeans.

Johnny sat at Piazza Beaubourg, rocking back and forth, his voice reverberating off the Pompidou glass. A group of Belgian teenagers were amassed before him, the boys and girls awed by his presence.

"Jah!" he shouted wildly. "Jah!" He bashed that guitar with all the fire in his belly, the ancient strings buzzing and falling short of pitch. His beer spilled and trickled down the paving stones, and he didn't even notice.

He had developed a singing style of broken reggae harshness, of a living booming instrument. The buttons on his coat scratched the pavement as he rocked, and he whistled through his teeth and clicked his tongue between phrases. His head moved, his legs moved, his dreadlocks danced about like a mop in a plug socket. He mixed English, French, and pure soulful scat. He shouted, he spat, he felt his shades press the bridge of his nose.

The Belgians watched entranced. The boys and girls sat wide-eyed, and their teacher sensed this was not an appropriate moment to herd them onward. He wracked his brain to find an educational aspect to this lunacy, but finding none whatsoever, decided to simply enjoy the sunshine instead, and leave his charges at it. His charges were in raptures, and were giving this bizarre African gentleman more attention now than he himself had received in over twenty years in the teaching profession. He smiled and de-fogged his spectacles.

Johnny finished the song and beamed widely. Glorious sunshine on his face, beads of sweat tickling. Where was this weather coming from in February? He'd abandoned the Pompidou early last December, as had become his custom during the winter, and hadn't expected to make a return till mid-March. But this – this was superb. The past two days had seen him leaning out the window on rue Leon, spitting down below and not believing the sun on the streets, until this morning he'd finally taken the plunge, and leaped over the metro barrier guitar and all, Beaubourg bound.

None of his associates were around when he got there, but feeling the energy in his bones once again, he just started singing when he found a place, in love and alive to the glory of the voice, lifting.

The Belgians left. A few of the girls tried to give him money, but he didn't want it or accept. They were only about fifteen, but pretty. He felt the burdening awareness of beautiful women, noticed the spilt beer can, and struck up another tune. Pigeons were around him, portrait artists too, but Johnny was again removing himself, eyes closed behind the impenetrable shades, the lust-heat of the physical ceding to the sound.

"C'est vraiment degueulasse ca," said someone, as Frank pissed between two parked cars. It was hot today, and he was drunk. The offended girl swivelled onwards, talking rapidly to a colleague. Frank eyed their departing backsides, pincered in the impotent rage of drink.

The heat shimmered in the air. There was dust and fumes. He walked purposeless, the can sloshing in his pocket, foaming. There was a tightness now within him, but he couldn't pinpoint where.

On he went to nowhere, hot and ill at ease. The sound and presence of other people caused disgust and irritation. Solitude brought mindless rage, and terror. He hurt most of the time. He hurt, and jittered. He walked the streets in agony, propelled forward by a hostile distant body. There was no wholeness or unity, because something had been breached.

Jackhammers ripped pavements, and dust and noise were constant. He was on rue Beaubourg, and up ahead was the enormous Centre Georges Pompidou. A jutting piece of Notre Dame lay further, across the river, scaffold-covered. He spat, and coughed, and spat again. Reached into his pocket and gulped messily. He took a right after Hotel de Ville, and walked riverside to Pont des Arts. Descended to the quai and pissed again, thirsty, sweaty, and hot.

The sun burned, next to Pont des Arts. He was directly in its glare. Two girls asked him for a light, and he was rude and didn't know why. The cruisers hummed past, and the water rolled like heaven. Homeless men climbed down from the beams that were their homes, and went to forage. He could see their sleeping bags and cardboard – makeshift domesticity, sentried by ravenous dogs.

Frank lay down, and tried to be still. There were people sunning themselves all along the right bank quai, and he eyed them gingerly. They didn't seem nearly as hassled by this glorious weather as he was. They didn't seem hassled at all. He stretched and shifted. He knew that whatever was wrong was getting worse.

24

Some days he felt so excited he just babbled randomly at strangers, but most days were so rotten he could lash out at a post-box. He stared skyward, and sighed.

He half-heard someone laughing, and his heartbeat quickened. He sat up abruptly, some memory reflex triggered, with it the damp feeling of nerves on a sunlit dental Tuesday. He probed his pocket for a tissue, and instead came out with a map of the Berlin U-Bahn. It was crumpled and frayed. It had parted from a lover, and he'd kept it ever since. Monica, from Italy. The stop names were familiar, but eerie too and foreign. Bismarck Strasse, Friedenau, Markisches Museum, Neukolln.

He looked at it carefully, following train lines, blinking in remembrance. The U7, the U6, the connection between the two at Mehringdamm. The Innenraum. Frank was hot and uncomfortable, but nostalgia was granting merciful relief.

He sighed and cried a little. Days before this torture, and awareness of futility. He blinked and sniffed, and attempted to relax his facial muscles, his shoulders moving up and down as he fought to align his breathing. He saw a seagull on the water. All the vacant dreams he had, and the dead weight of knowing they'd stay in his head. The U7 goes from Neukolln to Blisse Strasse, and he'd made that journey one time, with flowers in his hand.

Michel sat down beside him and they talked of this and that. Johnny wanted full payment for last time before he gave any more. He spat, and reminded Michel of his aversion to mixing business with pleasure. Coke was not discussed when the guitar was out. Coke was not dealt at Beaubourg. Coke was purely a minor activity to pay the bills, he was not a coke dealer, and if Michel wanted a coke dealer he, Johnny, was sure there were plenty to be found.

"Je suis chanteur," he barked. "C'est tout."

Michel, smiling to himself, shifted position on the ground. C'etait chaque jour la meme chose, and cajoling and haggling would be needed to derail Johnny's righteous conversation train, and still leave with the necessary. He lay down on his back. Johnny's guitar case served as a functional pillow, and he closed his eyes easily and thought of darling Karen, almost immediately beginning to worry after her well-being.

*

Karen walked the sunny street slowly, taking in the day sounds. Her stick tapped lightly. She held a bag of groceries in her left hand, and expected to be back at the flat around 11.40.
The morning air was sweet and pleasing. Friday, February 6th.

She was glad of this change in the weather, what with winter's wily treachery. Slippy and rushed, with invisible collisions potentially imminent, everywhere. Ice on pavements, and her stick could slip. Other people could slip, and hit her falling.

She reached her building and punched the code, and the lift brought her up to the third floor landing. Exit lift, turn left, first door on left. Her key had her name inscribed in braille – a gift from Michel. She turned on the tv, and could hear children squealing as they were remade as sexy popstars. Could hear their talk of favourite lipsticks.

Karen ate and listened to tv. Warmth on her face through the window. She turned down the sound, left the tv on, and heard birds. There was a plane flying somewhere overhead. With the television sound gone, the room settled into the atmosphere of daytime. The fridge hummed in the kitchen area. She turned the tv off, and there was stillness.

All alone in the afternoon, she finished the tuna. She exhaled and leaned back, slowly. Whenever Mom called it was to worry. Whenever Michel called it was the same. They'd never met one another, but in ways she felt they bore so much in common. They worried for her.

The sunshine threw crystals on the vase by the window, but Karen on the sofa doesn't care for light refraction. It isn't pertinent. Way back one time when, and she fell on the Chicago street, someone had expressed horror at all that red. Of course Karen knew what she was talking about, even as a little girl, but she'd decided quite soon after that colour didn't matter. Colour wasn't there. Yes her stick was white, and yes her hair was brown, but what's the use in knowing, if knowledge brings a blank. She stuck to the relevant, the pertaining. There was feeling, there was sound, there was touch and smell and moments. There was love. There was healthy eating and newspapers.

There is an exception to all of this. She got a glass of water and returned to the couch. Sat there thinking calmly. There is a photograph above, above Karen's head right now, in colour. It's there for all to look at, and for her to know it's there. It's framed. There is a boat out on a harbour, and distant glinting shoreline buildings, the sea all speckled randomly with golden frozen jewels. The camera-captured sun on the blue Lebanese ocean. "Fishing in Beirut," the taker called it.

Aria's new flat was in the 10th. She went up a cobbled street and down a tiny passage. When they got there she was sweating, and she threw down her bags and collapsed on the purple couch. She felt circular tingling throughout her body, with a strong pulse evident, hitting her bones in about six different places. She blinked and looked around.

Laura was glad Aria was here, because Marie had moved out five days previously, and she'd been sitting waiting for Aria's arrival ever since.

So had the landlord.

"We don't know why the weather's this hot," said Laura at the sink, dropping ice into two glasses of water. "It's been on the news and everything."

Aria drank slowly, and Laura sat beside her. They'd been friends since they were ten. Laura still worked in the restaurant she'd mentioned in emails, and the course at the Sorbonne still put all the emphasis on grammaire. Her boyfriend Lukas had turned out to be nothing but Swedish hairgel. A child bawled at her mother, audible now through the open skylight, and possibly audible at any other time also, and Aria smiled sadly, reminded of that baby on the plane.

She started to unpack, then left it, and lay down on her bed. She rubbed the surface, her nail catching the fabric. The bed was in a loft, not quite a separate room, up a ladder from the living area, and separable by curtain. Laura's was the same, in the other room, which contained a desk, a lamp, and a fair amount of the Spanish landlord's junk. Aria sat up from her bed, and could see traces of Selotape on the walls, where Marie must have put and removed her pictures.

Laura went to work, and Aria had pasta. Leaned out the window, and saw the neighbours leaning back. Her view was of a tiny courtyard – green trash cans about ten feet below, Arabic speaking women eyeing her curiously from windows opposite. She said Bonsoir, and one echoed it back, faintly.

She unpacked to low music. Sat still afterwards, awareness focused on her breathing and her heartbeat. The sensations of her body in this new place. She felt a wave of fatigue buck her, the muscles seemingly tightening and sagging all at once. She followed a tingling from her left cheek to her neck. Her head turned to the left, her wrists buzzing warm and ready. Warmth spread now, limbs and heart and soul, breathing coming freer, and teeth releasing tongue. She smiled, and yawned.

Sometimes in her mind she heard the clicking of the camera. Less than before, but sometimes. That oh so strange feeling positioned there before it – a feeling so exciting it was frightening and sore. A headlong wildness, and the genuine belief she was nearing some completion.
Her own body glowing, vulnerable for the lens, with the muttered dark instructions, talk of tits and ass and pussy.

The next day they saw the famous things. They took the metro to Anvers, and there was the Sacre Coeur. Aria was thrilled. It was crawling with sightseers, but the sun was high and clear, and together they gazed calmly at the shining Christian white. The city stretched before them as a rounded peaceful whole, looking ancient, perfect, and utterly deserted.

"I think it's great that you're here now," said Laura. "Better late than never."

Aria turned to look at her, the railing rubbing her arm, and they hugged right there in silence, below the tourists and the domes.

Montmartre was warm and quiet, the crowds of the Sacre Coeur left easily behind. They walked the streets in secrecy, ascending and descending steep steps. Birds sang songs of parochial self-containment, and the two American girls drifted, not caring to do more than walk alongside one another.

"It makes me think of home," said Laura. "Although it looks nothing like it."

One hour later, atop the Arc de Triomphe, Laura's phone rang. What followed was indecipherable to Aria, and not particularly like her language tapes. She strained to catch words and phrases, thinking she recognised some but not sure, and gazed down the Champs-Elysees at the trafficked lines of shining metal. Americans, Spanish, and Northern Europeans gazed with her. Laura got off the phone and they moved around the different sides. Put a coin in a creaking telescope. The streets came alive for Aria as she squinted, people and vehicles moving, like tranquil earth revealing teeming ant life in the eyepiece of a microscope.

Horns were occasionally audible. Shape and movement in the map-like distant streets. Laura took a turn to look, and Aria was asked to take a picture by a grinning Finnish couple. A child in a soccer jersey dashed past, too low to be caught in the viewfinder. She strolled around and looked west, the sun hitting the glass of the nearby La Defense skyscrapers, radiance held there like sheet metal, making her close her eyes and see red dots, flashing.

They clattered down the steps in the company of many, eyes needing to grow accustomed to the gloom. Back on the street, they craned their necks to where they had just been, other people mere specks up there now. Ice creams were in order. They sat down on a bench amid squealing tyres and Japanese tour groups. The men eyed them attentively, their near-identical plaid shirts holding pens, cameras, and foldable city maps. Their wives chatted absently. What words describe the sound of Japanese? They made memories for development, and set about the business of collective monument entry. The traffic circled crazily, on the world's first organised roundabout.

Aria and Laura spoke of San Jose. Of streets, incidents, and middle aged women with day-glo hair. Of high school. Laura said she never wanted to go back. They sat for a while, awoken to nostalgia, and stood up then in unison, and left.

Laura took Aria by Pont de Bir-Hakeim, because this is where Marlon Brando walked in Last Tango in Paris. They stood midway across, looking down at the tree-lined solitude of Allee des Cygnes. An old man sat on a bench hanging over the river, and the sun went in behind a cloud. Crossing the road to the other side, and remaining at the midway point, they stood in full view of the Eiffel Tower.

Laura took out her camera, and Aria stood in an alcove commemorating something she couldn't read. A light wind took up, the sky and water grey now, and her hair was fluttered gently. "So here's your big Paris photo," said Laura, the camera strap catching on the belt around her waist. A siren somewhere softly dopplered, and the American girl was snapped before the monument, in the sweet year of the Christian Lord, 2003.

*If your wishes are not granted, there's a chance you'll have to kill. Nobody wants to, but wrongs took place in history. Unholy acts were sanctioned. The French marched into his country, long before he was born, and they claimed it for themselves. They scorned as mindless his religion. He heard the stories growing up – the barbarism, the flame, the callous Western putdown of all it doesn't know.*

*More than one million lost in the War of Independence. Nearly two million more made instant refugees. Over one hundred years of French Imperial rule, and when they finally left, the country shook with pain. It was into this that he was born. The Western leaning authoritarian governments. The failure to uphold true Sharia law. The final humiliation came in nineteen ninety, when the holy Islamic party won legislative elections, and had their victory nullified. He was 14, and this was not too young to act. It was soon after they started calling him Djinn. Civil war began, chaos could bring change, and no one else made bombs for cars like the genie from the slums.*

*Their group was strong and certain, and members acted as they saw fit. They insisted on an Islamic state. They cut the throats of villagers, blew up foreign journalists, and left to suffer women who would not become temporary wives. They killed the blood kin of colons. Djinn wanted more. In the heat and dust of some deep Saharan bolt hole, he knew it couldn't end with simple government displacement. It was the French who had to pay. Hiding from his own military, a wanted man in a desecrated land, he began to search in earnest ways to flee and plot.*

*Passage to Lebanon came unexpectedly. A dark and terrible Mediterranean crossing, and a mad man in the galley screaming "Tell me where is Egypt!" He made it safely, and left that sorry ship behind. He is sitting in a sun-filled apartment, a space he shares with no one, in the Lebanese capital of Beirut. He has one knife, one fork, and two glasses. Three guns. Djinn spends hours by the window, thinking, watching, smoking cigarettes. It is calming.*

*In the middle distance is the bay, blue and dream-filled. He cannot see the Lebanon Mountains that rise to the east, behind him now, unless he goes up to the roof. He saves this for the evenings. For the eerie final sunsets on the jumbled tension city. On the Christian hills of Ashrafiyah, and Muslim Musaytibah. For the simple aching beauty of the white buildings in light. He has four shirts, two pairs of trousers. He has a watch with Western writing – mode, display, water resist.*

*He has been here two years. This apartment, this routine. Prayers in the morning and the evening. Traffic sounds are soothing, and silence speaks of peace. Allah expects duty to be done.*

*When the bomb goes off in Paris the world will finally listen. The plan is nearing completion. It has been gently coaxed from infancy, and is now a rumbling, almost real event. It has teeth, and claws, and the wisdom to carry itself through. When he speaks it aloud, he smells the smoke it will create. The building metal will soften, and the Western dogs will scream. He walks the streets for exercise, and gives the little children who live downstairs sweets and coloured pebbles.*

*Very often sunsets can make him want to cry. He doesn't cry of course, but wants to. The light embalms the stonework. The sky is magical, is perfect, is the glistening protection of the Middle Eastern kingdom. He stands on the roof in the evenings, looks to the eastern mountains, smokes and wants to cry. There are children sounds from the street below. Cooking utensils clatter in kitchens, open windows and murmurs of radio. Turn to the blue bay. Boats, the harbour, the odd unlikely tourist. The scars of civil war, and subsequent Israeli and Syrian occupation.*

*After this he returns to the window. Night falls, and he watches waking street lamps, with sweet mint tea slipping on his tongue.*

34

# BLUE
## July – September 2002

Cities are built by the strong, for the strong. Steps and kerbs hamper the disabled. Everything is motion and sound.

Frank is by the river. There's sweat on his brow, and there are sunbathers stretched randomly on the grass around. A man who works for the city is picking up rubbish, and the sprinklers wet the areas he has cleaned. There is a water skier out there, on the river, his cries and shouts carried easily ashore. Two girls and another boy are in the boat, laughing.

Frank watches all this, the cleaner and the surfer, the birds alighting easily, and the distant sun-haze policeman on the far bank, his shirt sleeves rolled up, with essentially no traffic to direct. Frank sees this man every day, or maybe it is different men and he can't tell, but he suspects it is the same one, always. He pulls from the joint, and the world seems sweeter, a bubble in a bubble, a crystal in a stream. The world feels vaguely sealed, and functioning.

There, across the water, is called Triana. It's long associated with gitanos. It's one of the oldest areas of the city, but Frank doesn't live there. He lives by the Alameda, by the flea markets and the smack, the tiny cervecerias and the winding, broken lanes.

Sevilla makes him feel like exploding. He doesn't stay still very long. He just moved here in June, and now it is July, with the squealing scooters and the 45-degree heat. He shares a flat with a French girl on calle Castellar, and has friends close by, in a house on calle Feria.

The walk to the river takes twenty-five minutes, and he does it every day, although it causes considerable distress. It's like exercising inside an oven. He trudges through the dead-heat streets, sweating, and feels anger rising in his soul. The ancient streets seem to wobble and constrict, and the old women eye the extranjero through callous wizened squints. His shirt like liquid skin.

He makes it every day though, and falls down in a sweat-heap, blinking. The river can generate a slight breeze, and this is worth a great deal when the apartment has no air conditioning. He sits beside the water.

Later he called for Dev. Dev and his girlfriend had a room in the calle Feria house, the house also containing a Dane, a Spaniard, an Argentinean and a Swede. Everyone spoke Spanish but Frank, all of them girls but Dev. Dev and Frank had gone to school together in Dublin, had smoked and drank and puked, and Frank had arrived in Sevilla about two months after Dev, eager for adventure after incapacitation.

They sat in the living room and sweated, two floors up in the thin rising house. Dev was wearing a pair of shorts and picking his nose.
"That kind of shit is like shooting ducks in a kettle," he said, "or whatever the phrase is. I mean it's just so easy that…who'd be bothered?"
Frank settled into his chair, relaxed, but fidgeting nonetheless.
Dev went and got two glasses of water.
"Do you want ice?" he said.
"Yeah."
He turned around and went back to the kitchen, and Frank heard the plop of the cubes in the glass.
"So how's the job?" asked Dev, reseating. For a week now Frank had been a morning cleaner in a fleabag hotel, revelling in the stillness of the dusty Spanish hallways. It was his calmest part of the day.
"It's alright. It's fine."
A cockroach scuttled across the floor. Dev seemed to think about reaching for the broom, but then slumped in a manner that suggested he couldn't be bothered, exhaling loudly. Frank rubbed a sweat-drop cascading down his nose.

They could stay like this for hours. A plate with bread crusts sat nearby, an empty glass previously containing milk. Clinging residue. Frank remembered hearing a glass used for milk can never be used for beer, no matter how many times it's washed. He eyed the glass carefully, nothing in its appearance suggesting awareness of a sober future. He sighed and rubbed his legs.

The Swedish girl came in and sat down. Frank couldn't remember her name, and Dev didn't use it in greeting. She sneezed. Frank wasn't sure if she was eighteen or in her late twenties, and his opinion on this changed with every passing moment. Her clothes were of a fifties style, but she was playing with a mobile phone. He didn't know if this was contradictory in a pleasing way or not.

"So Dev says you're cleaning a hotel," she offered, putting down the phone and looking at him full-on. Right then she was eighteen.

"Yeah, just in the mornings. It's fine."

"It's fine?"

"Yeah, it's alright y'know?"

He shifted in his seat. She seemed to be waiting for more.

"Jesus it's hot," said Dev, picking up a nearby guitar. "I can never tune this feckin' thing."

He handed it to Frank, who tuned it after a fashion, and handed it back. Dev started playing G and C and singing about a diner.

Sjal, for that was her name Frank suddenly remembered, listened carefully. Dev switched to a comedy falsetto, closed his eyes tight, and bashed the guitar like a bin lid. He shook his head and tapped his foot. This rhythmical tapping was accompanied by the swish of his leg on the couch. He screeched and shook. When he was finished, he splayed back into the softness, the guitar balanced upon him. Sjal clapped and Frank smiled. She thought he was funny, and Frank supposed he did too.

"And you play too?" said Sjal to Frank. "You were what do you call it for him."

"Tuning."

"Yeah, you were tuning for him. So you play too right?"

"Yeah," said Frank. "A bit."

"A bit? So will you play a bit then?"

Dev handed him the instrument, and Frank went to tune it again – an introduction, a prop, a way of readying himself.

He sang a song about a girl, a song he had written, a girl he hadn't known. The B string went flat at some point, but nobody cared. He finished and settled, smiling at the ground.

He felt pretty good. They went out for coffee, and Frank fell into a daydream. He moved his ankle about under the table to prevent stiffness. Stabs of pain were induced momentarily. "I wish I knew what you were thinking," said Sjal sweetly. "You seem to just go off sometimes."

He knew he liked her, but nothing as simple as that. Not the easy beauty of courtship. He didn't want to impress her, he didn't want to try. It was like discovering a relative, a connection of blood and outlook. He moved his ankle, and wasn't sure what to think.

They lay in bed together. Softness. She felt his breath against her right cheek, and moved closer. Was he sleeping or not? "Michel?" she said gently, not wishing to wake him if he was sleeping.

"Hmmm," he murmured.

She got up for a glass of water. The sound of the tap. It touched her lips in coolness, the water from the tap, and in her mouth, in her throat, the fullness and the peace.

She returned to him. Pulled the sheet over her body, their bodies, and lay still. She thought of that junk tv, sitting in an old box in the living room, and it probably wouldn't even work when she tried to plug it in. Why she took it she couldn't say. That poor old man, Boulier, his leathery face and calming foyer touch. His paternal grace.

"Bonjour Mademoiselle, il fait beau aujourd'hui, non?" His laugh, and his fingers on her wrist.

Karen cried in bed, the Monday morning news of his death absorbing up to this point, and now being accepted. The tears released the pain. She cried on this Wednesday afternoon, and Michel slept alongside, his easy nasal breathing a partner to her sobs.

Johnny was selling a lot today. Things were going so fast he felt like he was on the stuff himself. He jumped up and down, bug-eyed, yanking the phone out of his pocket and speaking in code to people on the other end. They were always saying they'd know the final order in an hour.

"Je ne peux pas attendre," he hissed, again and again. "Dis-moi" He was sweating, and he sensed his agitation may be growing apparent to those around him.

Tourists were gaping, and not at the Centre Pompidou. He was going to have to cool it. He looked around, the building's blue pipes blurring as his head swivelled, the pipes and the tourists and the crepe smell and this fucking guy in his ear all mashing into one bizarre sensory experience, his stress refusing clarity.

He stuffed the thing back in his pocket and sat down. He really wanted to play something loud about now, to shout and rock and whistle, but he was too frazzled, and then the unholy thing went off again.

He leapt up like he was on fire, cursing and answering at the same time. He put his shades in his pocket with his left hand. The guy told him he wasn't sure at this moment, because he had to talk to "some people," but he'd know in an hour.

"Fuck you Yank!" Johnny screamed, unaware of how this man could even have his number, or who he was. "You have a wrong number. Do not call again!"

He hung up and sat down, but then stood up to swap the contents of his pocket, reseating with the phone in the pocket and the shades on his head. His face contorted into a grimace of dismay and confusion.

"I don't know," he said to a passing child.

"I really do not know."

Later he felt better. Some of the heat went out of the day, and he sang a few songs to ease the tension. He winked at two Japanese toddlers.

The buttons of his coat scraped the guitar as he strummed, the whole thing covered in random marks and scratches.

"Why?" he roared. "Why ayayayayayay?"

People came and sat with him. Some he knew. A joint was passed, a champagne bottle went pop, and he left this hippy girl in charge of the guitar to go and buy crisps and bread.

He kneaded his fingers as he walked to the shop, feeling alright now, and noticing some white guy in a Senegalese jersey. Dakar back streets, but that wasn't today nor yesterday. He banished the thought. The hot July night came swooping, and he made it back to the group and sat down. All this energy around, and he had that twitch in his groin. He looked about and clicked his tongue, thought about resting an arm on the girl beside him, but didn't. Her laugh was not conducive. She was laughing here, having fun, and he could never put the moves on a certain type of joy. Disappointment was a target, innocence was not. It was terrifying.

He rubbed his nose and checked his messages, and there was one, but he couldn't be bothered reading it. He put it back in his pocket. A few pigeons remained, strutting and bickering low, and he watched them momentarily, before closing his eyes.

*"Why have you left me lonely?*
*Why have you made me cry?*
*Why have you left me lonely?*
*Why ayayayayay..?*

Frank and Sjal and Dev ate olives. It was another sweltering day. They were at an Alameda café, and a heroin addict who used to be a ballerina was floating about for change. Sjal gave her something. A child threw a tomato on the ground in a tantrum, and his parents weren't overly concerned. He wanted chocolate instead.

Frank had a fair amount of chocolate in his back pocket, but not like the kid wanted, and himself and Dev smoked some discreetly. A stalling car engine burst up in flames. There were shouts of surprise from the driver, hurling himself from his vehicle, pleading in his eyes for someone to approach. Their waiter strolled over with an extinguisher.

The event aroused interest for about thirty seconds, and then everyone forgot and went back to whatever. Frank watched carefully. The burn smell was in the air, in the hot already burning air, and he ate another olive, and gazed at the poverty and dust. The man was thanking the waiter, "gracias, gracias," and this in itself was unusual, because nobody in that city says thanks.

"Vale," said the waiter, and walked off.

"Is anybody hungry?" said Dev.

Sjal ate an olive.

"Hungrier than this I mean." He swung back in his chair and yawned. "I'd love a big roast chicken and spuds. With gravy and peas and carrots."

Sjal eyed him in amazement, and Frank laughed softly, bemused and amused at once.

"Feckin' roast spuds as well," said Dev. "And stuffing."

He made an exaggerated lip smacking sound, and then a moan of pleasure, and spat an olive stone back into the world.

"Spuds and stuffing and chicken. Ya can't bate it."

So they went for food, but sandwiches and crisps – Dev's mind far bigger than his belly. Sjal didn't eat meat. She told them she had lived in Paris, had seen a lot of great films there, and once found a key ring on the Boulevard Saint Michel.

She took it out, and it was a pink bear that lit up when she pressed a button. They couldn't see this very well, but she semi-covered it in her hand and it was better.

It was made of a glass-like plastic, and had a red dickie-bow. Frank and Dev held it. Handing it back, Frank thought he thought something, but then dismissed it. He turned away with a frown. She put it back in her pocket, and Dev stole one of her crisps.

That night there was a flamenco show, a cantankerous affair of wailing and death, and they sat there drinking, Frank rotating his ankle muscles again and again, a cracking sound audible. Today had been tough, and the pain was acute now. Sjal adored this music, was spellbound and moving and light, her duende eyes dancing also, both yearning and pulsing at once. She took a drink and ate a peanut.

Dev got up for beer. The music grew more intense, a cathartic clenched cacophony, and Frank watched in wonder, as Sjal swayed. She was there and not there also. Almond eyes, and a young face lined with faint anxiety, from thought upon thought upon thought. Her knuckles were tapping the table. She turned to look at him then, but he felt he couldn't be seen, and maybe in her trance-state she detected the system breach. His hollowness in need. This was July and sweetness, the damage a year before, and Frank in Spanish night-time doesn't know what is to come. He's had the pain, the repair, the physical re-knitting of the cartilage and bone. But the thunder hasn't rolled yet, the soul has not yet screamed, and the sense of dislocation has just begun to loom.

The dog was on the roadside. His tongue fell from his mouth in a perfect expression of defeat, and his blood stained the tarmac in a semi-circular arc. A dead dog in the dream time. Flies were buzzing - landing, invading, and raw, and Aria stood sadly. Heat haze rose about, shimmering and delicate, and she put her hand to her mouth, child-like, deriving shallow comfort from a stance of blue compassion.

She stepped down onto the beach. This time one week ago she should have been landing in Paris, but she wasn't ready yet. Laura had understood. Aria had made enormous strides recently, but it was still a little soon to just jump on a plane and go live somewhere new. She pushed back her hair and breathed deeply.

Gulls darted overhead. There were people visible in the middle distance, the tide way out, and the people out there also, walking, scattered, where the ocean licked the land. She could turn around and see occasional traffic, or could re-focus her attention on these dot-like figures, but neither image allowed for sound accompaniment. She heard nothing but her own breathing and footsteps, and the circling overhead birds.

Her trainers were caked in sand. It was wet, slushy, a heavy clinging sea-sludge, and the sky was overcast now, although the humidity remained. There were little marks in the sand-surface, where worms had buried and emerged, with speckled greyish seashells arranged in random curves. She rubbed her foot against the matter.

The grey-white sky was purposeful. Enormous bags of raindrops, hovering, intent, waited to spill and batter, with Aria below. She looked up and pushed hair from her eyes. Someone had dropped a can, a red one, and it lay there in the sand, half-covered and rusting. She went to pick it up but didn't. All alone with her breath and her body, she realised how far she had come, how distant now was the panic and the fear, the incapacitating nausea of just a few months earlier. How sad she felt for what she had done.

Then she did pick up the can. She held it aloft, motionless, and cried.

Dev spat an olive stone.

"They're addictive these things," he spluttered. "This is my third jar today." Frank had made soup in his apartment, but he had no idea why, as the two of them sat there eating, sweating for God and country. It was siesta in Sevilla.

"So they made you sweep the parts you'd already swept?" said Dev. "Just to be doing something."

"Yeah."

"For fucks sake."

Frank pushed away his soup bowl and wiped his brow.

"It wasn't even dirty in the first place," he muttered. "They don't have any fucking guests."

Dev sat up and rolled a joint. A big cone that could floor an elephant. He folded, rolled and licked, his tongue protruding from the left side of his mouth, like an eager child engrossed in what he was doing.

They smoked in silence.

"When I was about six," said Dev, "I got my first erection. This wasn't in the gaff my parents have now, it wasn't in Dublin. It was when I was a kid, in Navan. It was summer, really hot – not as hot as this obviously, but y'know, hot. I was in the garden, or we were in the garden I should say, cause it was me, Johnno, and PJ. Jesus, fuckin' PJ. Last time I saw him he was on parole. Anyway, yeah, we were in the garden yeah, me Johnno and PJ, and y'know, summers day, I think we had ice-cream or something. I was six. Anyway, the next-door neighbour was out sunbathing, like, in her garden, and I mean, fuck, what a fuckin' slapper. Lying there real kind of, I don't know…there was only a little fence between the two gardens. I couldn't see over, but I could see through. She was lying out there, covered only in a towel, and I mean, it was obvious to us, through the fence at six years old, that there was nothing underneath. I'd say she was about thirty.

Anyway, she's lying there, we're watching, and the thing is, she knew we were watching, y'know? She knew. So…what does she do? She takes off the towel. This is Navan, 17, 18 years ago. And she knew we were watching, y'know?

She takes off the towel, lies there, totally naked, and we were watching through the fence, and, I mean, we had never seen anything like that before. She was about thirty I'd say, and she wasn't bad. But what a fuckin' slapper, y'know? To get your thrills from doing that. And that was the first time. Just lying there, y'know..?"

Frank laughed. So did Dev. Frank glanced at him, and he was giggling and smoking. A scooter went by outside, a churning headwreck growl, and Frank's knee flinched in sudden shock from the sound.

Dev stood up and went to the window. He spat down below. Frank finished the smoke and stubbed it out, wiping tobacco entrails off the table with his left hand. They rained slowly toward the floor, a waterfall of matter, a tumbling little shower that the ground was calling home. He spied an ant and squashed it.

"Sometimes I don't know about this fuckin' place," said Dev, his voice half muffled with his body leaning out. "It's a bit of a shithole to be honest."

He laughed again, easy and fine with himself, and Frank smiled also, because the man by the window was right.

"So leave," he taunted gently, standing up to stretch, and he moved toward the window where Dev was leaking spit.

"Leave for somewhere new."

"I might," said Dev, dribbling, laughing and foaming and mad, his body now suspended over a twisting cobbled street.

"I could leave and go to Holland, and never go back home, and draw and smoke and dance, just like nature intended."

He spat down below, and laughed as he wiped his chin.

Karen dressed in silence. She had awoken in plenty of time, and dressed with deliberation, the day all fresh and new.

She ate the muesli, drank the fruit juice. The washing of the breakfast implements took two minutes, and she placed them back in their drawers and shelves and presses. She wiped down the surface. Her mother leapt into her mind. She wiped the surface and did battle with her mental mother, but then cut loose and suppressed these thoughts. She put the cloth in the sink.

The morning feel was soothing, imbuing her with a sense of calm. She brushed her hair and teeth, combated wrinkles and dryness, and applied lipgloss and perfume.

She was ready to leave the flat. The lift hummed in old familiar compliance, and she reached the bottom and the street. A bus or something roared by. She swept the ground with her stick, advancing easily, mounting and dismounting kerbs and steps. So Karen, in her time, reached the St. Sulpice metro.

She was never at her most comfortable on these trains. Of course they were fine, nothing had ever gone wrong, not really anyway, but they were firmly classed under necessary evil, and she took a bus, or buses, if time or route would allow.

She sat there amidst the rattle and the din. The human noise of coming, going, shifting, talking was everywhere. She had thirteen stops, heading north, before she got to Chateau Rouge. She was on an errand for Michel.

She had met this man before. Once, at Christmastime. She had touched his weary face, had heard his rumbling voice. Had listened to the rasp while he murmured in his phone. He would be here now, at the Chateau Rouge metro station, because he had stuff for Michel, and Michel was in Bordeaux. The call had come the night before. Michel, sweet, pleading, on the phone from his parents house, with his *please, it would mean a lot. Collect some stuff from this guy, you remember him. I can't make it back, and he says he can't wait.* Karen had wondered why, where was the urgency in this, but Michel said I don't know, and he'd sounded so sincere.

**48**

So here she was on the train. Friday morning. They got off, they got on, they shuffled here and there, finding seats and excusing themselves. She was sure some eyes were on her. This was the tenth stop she counted, so this was Gare de l'Est, with three more to go. She thought of the El back in Chicago, those childhood trips downtown with her mother, and then later with friends, or alone. The strangeness of her first drink.

She remembered just how cold, just how to the bone freezing, that city got, and however bad Paris was, ice and snow in Chicago made for nightmares without end. Temperatures of death, and streets of crystal traps.

The train reached the stop. She moved through the exit door, and people pushed past, surging, the many who don't pay and evade the dumb control. She heard others jumping over the barriers.

Coming up the stairs and into the day, the sound of markets was everywhere. Her left hand gripped the rail. There was the feel of other bodies, other human beings, clambering about. The heat of breathing souls. As she reached the final step, she heard a sudden cough, and turned to face this man, knowing who it was.

Sjal twirled the liquorice. It was red and black and sugar frosted, and seemed to hold more appeal as an accessory than food. She laughed and placed it down. Frank sat opposite, no drink before him as he'd just arrived, sweating and sore after walking from the river. They were at a café right outside her house.

It had been a strange moment, as he walked down the road in the stress heat, the ravaging extreme, and there she had appeared, dressed in red and white, looking cool, at peace, and quite content to see him. He'd sat down and dropped bread he'd bought on the pavement. She drank her café solo and they talked of coloured string, the subject not as vital as the joy of words to say. They laughed at misunderstandings. Frank ordered nothing, the waiter never appeared, and the advancing clock pleasingly subdued some of the sun's excess. She told him about Malmo.

He played with an unopened sugar pack. He learned of a connecting bridge between her city and Copenhagen. Spanish voices passed. She asked things about Dublin, was curious and real, and he answered like a teacher, and wasn't quite sure why. He said the only Spanish word he knew was casa.

She said friends of hers were coming soon. One would be here in a few days, and would be staying who knows how long, with two others coming later, and staying just a week. Friends from Stockholm. The sugar conga'd in the packet like sand in an African shaker, as he shook it up and down rhythmically. The car they'd seen on fire lurched down the street, the bonnet black and pockmarked, a veritable hazard to the occupant and anyone else in the vicinity. Frank checked his bread was still there.

Aria spoke to Laura on the phone. Her mother would not be happy with the expense. Laura had recently met a guy called Lukas, and cooed down the phone as Aria just laughed. He was a writer.

"So when do you think it will be possible?" Laura asked.

"Soon," said Aria. "Soon. I think maybe a few months, or a little longer."

"That's cool. I'll be here."

Aria twirled the phone cord, and felt happy and sad at once. She knew that she was mending, but memories remained. Would they always? She ran her foot along the kitchen floor, moving back and forth, speaking low to Laura, who'd never let her down. Tears welled. She cried and laughed while talking, so good to hear this voice, the promise of the future all sweet and almost real. They laughed like little kids. The cat appeared beside her, blinking and relaxed. It yawned its peaceful greeting, the way it always did.

"So tell me how you're feeling, I really want to know."

Aria told her, was not ashamed with Laura, did not feel wrong or dirty, or sickened by her past. Light played on the lino, engulfing the cat as the day wound on, and they talked without remission, so much to hear and tell. Her mother came back, wasn't angry at all really, and let them keep on talking, to see her daughter smile again.

Aria felt so happy. So tingling, shining happy, talking to her best friend on another continent. Already this moment was crystallising, being stored deep somewhere warm, because she knew while in it how truly great it was. She was remembering and experiencing at once. She felt the cuffs of her sweater against her wrists, paid attention to this while talking, and noticed her body growing warmer, more relaxed. A stiffness seemed to melt. She moved her neck and shoulders, and placed full awareness on her cheek against the phone. The fridge touched her elbow.

Laura said something in French. Aria was momentarily confused, but then Laura explained that some guy was asking how much longer she was going to be.

Aria tried to imagine the view from a Parisian payphone standing in her kitchen. She was sure image and reality didn't match.

"Anyway," said Laura, "I won't stay too much longer. Now there's an old woman behind that guy who was hassling me. I'm causing a jam."

Aria heard the sound of other voices. They said their goodbyes to one another, ending with a promise to be together soon. Aria listened to the line going dead before she herself hung up. The city of Paris shrunk into nothingness, her portal having closed, the living breathing difference no longer hers to hear. She stood silent in America.

An empty cereal packet lay on the counter, with a smiling cartoon character holding out a spoon. She ate this stuff for comfort, and the cat played with the box. Aria stayed inert, the day pulsing around, and felt a little tickle deep behind her nose. One time they'd made her cut her toenails, when they were too long. They'd waited behind the camera as she did so. She heard a bird through an open window, but not from the kitchen; from a window open somewhere in the daytime rhythm house. She saw dust peeping out under the fridge.

The cat rolled on his back, shimmied across the lino, and scratched playfully at her jeans. His belly was soft and exposed. She watched in affection. Truth is both big and everyday she thought, profound and commonplace, and sunlight on a surface is as pure as burning hope. To travel, to care, to love and to be loved, to nurture one another in the darkness and the pain. Things are hardest at the point of desire.

Johnny cut the powder. He chopped lines, and she snorted it from his bed, half-covered by a faded African rug. She was scarred across her breast. Why he let her come here he didn't really know, but mostly when she called he was prone to answer yes. It was easier.

Her hair was blond but darkening, and her hands shook involuntarily. She called him J. The rug was across her belly and thighs, and she was sitting in a lean, her left arm on the dirty mattress for support. He had four lines done on the back of a book, and he handed it to her.

"Je pense parfois que tu me detestes," she told him. He reassured her she wasn't hated. There was someone calling on the street outside, and Johnny bade her be silent till he strained to hear if it was for him. Satisfied it was not, he reseated.

"Cover up your tits," he said roughly, and she scowled and did so. The rug was now exposing her thighs, and he exhaled in frustration and jumped up, clicking his tongue and fingers simultaneously. From a drawer he fetched a tablecloth, threw it at her fast, and when she failed to move, he draped it across her legs. Now she was head and feet.

"J'ai trop chaude maintenant," she murmured. He rolled his eyes and removed the cloth. She kicked her legs as if they had just been freed, and he reached over to knead her calf. She purred from somewhere sad.

"Oui bebe," she offered low, and his hand went slightly up. He continued, advanced, stroked the pallored skin. She lay back.

His phone rang. He thought about ignoring it, but then he picked it up, and talked of drugs and money with his right hand in the girl. She twisted while he spoke.

"All of that is not possible at once," he said. This guy sounded English, and had his number from Michel. Johnny was going to have to talk to Michel. He stood up abruptly, and she hit him with her foot, a hiss of sharp annoyance pushing from her mouth. He batted the foot away and removed himself to the window.

"Next week," he said to whoever. "Next week will be OK."

Two children were playing football down below. An African and a Turk, judging by the latter's jersey. The World Cup had just ended, Brazil the champions since June 30. Johnny watched the kids volleying. He didn't want to see his room, her body, the drugs and books and guitar strings, everything strewn about randomly. He wanted to watch this. Soccer. Football. Wholesome activity. Zidane and Figo, and the pursuit of excellence. His call ended, and he stared, transfixed.

The ball bounced on the concrete. The children passed with skill. He wanted to be down there, to be running, to be sweating from exertion as the muscles pumped. To be asexual and uncaught. To never know lust, desire, betrayal or relief. To be the man who runs with the ball. To have no knowledge of women, of drugs, of the mechanics of the city. To kick and sweat in peace.

He heard her calling his name.

"J," she whispered. "J, viens ici. Je suis desolee."

He turned back to reality.

Walking over gently he climbed on to the bed, and she worked on his belt as he pushed off the rug. The springs creaked in protest, the bed so old and bent. They lay side by side, hands exploring skin, and when she kissed his lips, he felt his soul relax. The ball skidded off the kerb outside.

Sjal's friend arrived. She was smaller, blonder, a cynic with a heart, and she took to caring for everyone with gruff maternal pride. Her name was Pernilla. She shook hands with Frank upon introduction, did not kiss his cheek, and wanted Sjal to confirm the English sentences she made, although they were perfect. Frank felt her eyes held distant secrets.

The three of them, along with Dev's girlfriend Beth, went to the cinema, and then to the bar where Dev worked. Frank's mind swam with the film he had seen. The story concerned an Italian actress, and had been written and directed by an Italian actress, who was herself playing the lead. It was shot on digital cameras.

This character was a star in Italy, and was desperate to make a film, which shared its title with the film on the screen. Her life was a tumultuous crash of drugs, parties, and abuse, most of it self-inflicted. The film was jagged, sprawling, egocentric and sublime, with dreams, violence, and desperate, lonely sex. It was a broken masterpiece.

Frank had been struck by his feelings for this girl, because for what girl? Was this person playing herself? The film seemed to suggest it was but a fictional documentary, reality thinly disguised, and if this was true, Frank wanted to find this girl and hold her tight. To push gently the hair from her tear-stained eyes.

He took out the hand-written copy of a poem he'd read and transcribed for keeping. He carefully smoothed the page.

*'Andamos*
*sobre un espejo*
*sin azogue,*
*sobre un cristal*
*sin nubes.*
*Si los lirios nacieran*
*al reves,*
*si las rosas nacieran*
*al reves,*
*si todas las raices*

*miraran las estrellas*
*y el muerto no cerrara*
*sus ojos,*
*seriamos como cisnes.'*


What it meant he couldn't say. Pernilla and Sjal spoke in Swedish beside him, and Beth watched Dev, as he poured and served cervezas. Frank listened to the Scandinavian tongue. It was German but wasn't, was Dutch but wasn't, though Dutch was closer than Deutsch. He had never heard it before.

He put the poem back in his pocket. He had been tempted before to ask Sjal for a translation, but had always refrained. It might lose something in the meaning. His glass was nearly empty, but the girls had plenty left, so he sat there in the evening, and listened while they spoke. They laughed and joked together. "Can you understand any of this?" asked Sjal. "Maybe we should speak in English."

Frank said he didn't, but they should speak whatever they liked. She said they liked speaking English, and so he asked what she thought of the film. She sat thinking carefully, considering either her opinion or how to phrase it, and Frank felt Pernilla watching, weighing up for herself the nature of this friendship. He took some of Sjal's beer.

"It was quite hard to relate to," said Sjal. "For me anyway. Her life was totally removed from mine, basically in every way, and for that reason I felt really far from it. So I'm not sure what I thought."

Pernilla said she liked it more. Said she understood it. Frank had known this would be so, despite having just met her, and he watched carefully as she tried to articulate her feelings without mentioning whatever personal references she may have had. She was skirting something dark.

Frank got more beer for everyone, because if they didn't drink it, he would. The night consolidated, evening light now gone. Dev served beer to Americans who couldn't have been more than sixteen, their attempts to be adult failing to disguise the pure light of incredulous excitement.

Frank and the girls drank slowly, needing to be nowhere else. Dev disappeared for a while to change a keg. The Cruzcampo beer was relaxing if it was anything, or it certainly was that night. Frank felt happy right in the moment. Sjal and Pernilla spoke of their friends' imminent arrival, in English, telling Frank their names and interests. Lise and Mette. He laughed at all these names, and they laughed at him for laughing.

Dev came back and stopped working, what with hardly any customers now and two other bar staff on duty. He splashed a beer down beside the others.
"This place is terrible isn't it?" he said, looking around and clicking his tongue in disdain. "Sometimes I want to start throwing things, just to see what'll happen."
He laughed, and swivelled his head with a manic look in his eyes.
Beth drank from his glass.

Pernilla asked Dev to tell a story. He cleared his throat, and looked at Frank to share the humour. He had a glint in his eye.

"Let me see now," he began, lapsing into pure country shtick. "Sure what feckin' stories would I know?"

The Swedes were enchanted already, and Dev knew it, and in that moment Frank was reminded of how good a friend he really was, and always would be.

"I remember one time when I was back on the farrrrrrrrrm," said Dev, tugging at imaginary braces, "and there was a feckin' goat that needed milkin' quare fast. Jaysus, them were the fuckin' days, y'know."

Frank knew that Dev's farming experience was limited to one school trip, but he naturally made no mention of this. Dev warmed to the theme.

"Anyway, this feckin' goat, yeah. He never liked me. He never liked me one feckin' bit I tell ya." He smiled warmly. "He was an oul bollox."

The girls were in stitches, and Beth and Frank basically were too, though they'd heard this stuff many times before. Dev kept catching Frank's eye.

"So I walk up to him, yeah," said Dev, " this oul bollox of a goat. And he's givin' me the evil eye."

He cleared his throat again, and took a swig that would put out a fire. He swished it around his mouth.

"And I says to him; 'what's wrong with ya? Sure don't ya need milkin' quare fast?' And he stands there lookin', the evil eye fixed on me like a gun."

"But surely you can't milk a male goat," said Sjal, and suddenly everyone realised how ludicrous this story really was. It seemed to Frank that Dev had only become aware of this aspect as well. He laughed and drank more beer.

"I dunno," he said. "I wouldn't say you can. But there's a first time for everything, y'know?"

So they finished drinking and left the bar, going somewhere else for wine and coffee. They passed the cathedral all bathed in lights. Moorish and Christian building, vying to praise the Lord, and tourist maps for money, all scattered on the ground.

Sjal and Pernilla spoke gently in their Swedish, and nobody else said anything at all.

Michel had been apologising for a week. He had sent flowers, brought flowers, had turned up unannounced with chocolates, wine, and bread. She was beginning to thaw. She knew this, was consciously aware of it, but felt fine, and had no more use for anger. She let him in on the seventh day.

He thanked her profusely, rubbing her hand in his. She smiled from the weight of affection. She no longer wanted to ask what that package was, no longer even cared. It was good to have him back, and good to feel his hand.

He insisted on using his English, and she listened and didn't correct.

"I have been speaking with my mother yesterday," he said. She boiled the kettle and reached for cups, and he took coffee and she tea. His mother had asked after her.

He went to the kitchen for more sugar, and right then the thought rose again. What had it been? She suppressed it after a second. He returned, sat down, and she felt herself stiffen as his leg touched hers. She did battle with her anger, wanting to feel nothing but joy. She had thought this was behind her, but... Why had he sent her up there for some package? Begged her to go, and meet this guy. She was baffled and still upset.

She heard him drinking beside her. Michel Rigaudeau. He slurped his coffee gently, in a way that was normally endearing, and today she wanted to like it too, but couldn't. She had to be honest with herself, and admit she was still resentful. She sighed and drank some tea.

"So how is your mother doing? Had she anything else to say?"
"No, not really. I think that mostly she was just to say hello. Oh, and that she has bought a new car. From German."
"Germany." She couldn't help herself.
"Yes, that's right. Germany."

Karen drank more tea.
"I have always liked this picture," he said. He must have been looking at the wall behind. "I like the water, and the boats, and the...how do you call the sun when it's in water?"

"The reflection.""Ah yes, of course. The reflection. Yes, this I like." She heard the fabric of his jacket scratching, as he turned back around beside her. Then he took off the jacket, and placed it on the sofa arm. She listened as he folded it carefully.
His leg started jumping, and he sniffed and rubbed his nose. She put a hand on the leg, exasperated. These French boys could be children.

They were silent for a while, and she took her hand away. She listened to her fridge. The gentle easy buzzing always put her mind at rest. She sat back, loosening her shoulders. Yes, that picture on the wall, she liked it too, and this man beside her also. She breathed deeply. She re-placed her hand, the warmth of his knee assuring, and they sat together on the couch, in daytime.
"Je veux etre avec toi," he whispered. "Je t'adore."

She put her head on his shoulder. There are moments to be angry she thought, and moments to be soft, and she touched his face, his neck, in softness. Comfort from skin. Curling into him further, she smelled his familiar smell, and Michel who'd made her travel became Michel who made her safe. They were together in a simple moment, entwined, and hurt and dislocation seemed to melt like passing snow.
Hot Parisian summer.

Aria ate quietly. After, she washed the spoon and bowl, and replaced them where they belonged. She stepped outside. The garden was bathed in sunlight, some clothes hanging on the line. She smiled at the sight of her little sister's pyjamas. When she was fourteen she had crouched out here in the darkness, smoking a Marlboro Menthol with Laura they had taken from her mother. Coughing and spluttering.

She looked around and kicked gently at the grass. A radio could be heard from the neighbour's. Every now and then the feel of the sea entered the garden, and it did so now, wonderfully. She breathed salty air. She went over and touched the clothes, kneading them in her palms to check for dampness. None remained. Her sister's pyjamas, her own T-shirts and jeans. Her mother's red blouse. All were dry and flapping.

Clothes feel different. From each other, and in wet and dry states. She felt it would be possible to correctly identify her T-shirts, blind-folded. Possible with practise and awareness. Aria closed her eyes and experienced the fabrics, the clothes on the line in the garden. She stood on sun-warmed grass.

She was thinking of Paris all the time now, and took this as a sign of further improvement. The future seemed very real again. She rubbed her tongue over her teeth, and could taste the remnants of cereal. Sugar and mushed up wheat. A bird alighted on the grass nearby, a magpie. One for sorrow unfortunately, but then it was joined by another, and she laughed out loud at this lucky spectacle.

"What are you thinking?" asked her mother.

Aria hadn't heard her approach, but wasn't startled.

"Oh nothing, just thinking."

Her mother drew up alongside, and smiled, ruffling her daughter's hair. All of this had been hard on everyone.

The magpies took off, one and then the other, and her mother squeezed her shoulder gently.

"Two for joy honey."

"I know it," said Aria, and they took each other's hand. Sweet breeze ruffled grass.

"You'll be able to go soon you know."

"I know."

"The past won't even matter."

Aria was amazed by her mother's strength. The shock of what she'd learned and dealt with. Her daughter had been driven to a shadow world of pain. Was it because of Benny? The absent father, who had left so long ago. Hollow, desperate, amateur photography - sad, explicit poses. Aria, attempting to repair the breech of childhood night abuse. Mother and daughter had been forced to educate themselves on trauma, but had emerged stronger, clearer. Despite the sometime ache, the past contained the worst. Aria had reclaimed herself.

The cat joined them in the garden, and little Anna too, just dropped home by a neighbour. Eight year's wise, a pretty little girl, jumping and laughing on the grass. Describing her day in detail. Pictures and games at summer school.

They all stood together, a broken family no more, and early next year the eldest daughter would leave for France. Aria plaited Anna's hair. What promise in the Parisian air - what would happen, who would she see? A white cloud drifted by, looking like an oval, or maybe like a plane. Yes, looking like a plane, singing softly of possibility. Anna counted her knuckles.

Frank swept the hallway. The owner shuffled by, muttering something he didn't catch, and Frank made no attempt to make him repeat it. Sunlight cast a golden square on the tile. The dust rose and danced, aroused by the brush in the morning. The bristles whispered and hissed.

The owner returned, and seemed to repeat himself. Frank stared blankly.

"Mas fuerte!" spat his boss. "Mas fuerte!" He made muscular sweeping motions himself. "Venga, venga!"

Frank told him to fuck off in his mind, but worked with more vigour for the next thirty seconds, till the man ceased observing him and disappeared around a corner. The he stopped and wiped his brow.

"Fuck off," said Frank. Sweat glistened on his fingers. He thought of that girl in the Italian film, the dark-haired wild one, with the slow siren smile. He leaned heavily on the brush. The dust settled in the sun square. He resumed sweeping, disturbing particles once more, and thought of the cheese sandwich that would soon grant respite. Cheese and sugary Spanish bread.

He completed the hall and stopped. Not one guest had passed all morning. In the stillness he heard a faint clock-tick, and listened to his breathing intermingling with the sound. Then this disturbed him, and he coughed. He rubbed his tired eyes. Sjal had told him that the eyes were the windows to the soul, but all windows need closing sometimes. He yawned in the hot lazy morning.

He finished up soon after. He walked back to his flat, climbed the stairs to his door, and gave himself a panic attack trying to fit the key in the lock. He was confused and momentarily terrified, and he frantically sought a reason while he reassured himself. This happened now occasionally.

He knew what it was. It was the feel of his pulse pumping hard in his neck, which was a natural occurrence after three flights of stairs, but was today disconcerting in the heat of Sevilla. He called round to Dev, shaky and twitching.

Dev poured water and listened carefully. He understood, and Frank knew this, for Dev had once been beaten severely, and his real work had only begun after the physical recovery. He folded his arms and breathed out.

"You know I understand this," he said. "And so I only say this now, because I know that you know I'm not talking through my hat. But it's ourselves who give us the fear. And deep in your heart you know that. The head-rushes, the panic, your mind telling you something terrible's coming. It's fucking awful. But listen to what I learned. Don't waste a second of this life worrying about things that might befall you. Not a fucking second Frank. The energy can be better used, and there's nothing worse than feeling frightened of being afraid."

He sat back and drank some water.

"It takes a long time, y'know?"

The girls were expected tonight. Lise and Mette, Sjal's other friends. Frank knew this, and realised he had actually been counting the days since first hearing of them. If he was honest with himself he was excited. He was back in his flat now, feeling better after talking with Dev, and Beth had told him to call to the house at ten. They would be there by then, and what with Sjal and Dev working, she'd joked of wanting all the help she could get. Frank was shelling a nut.

The tv was on, showing the bullfights. He watched these in horror and awe. It was dreadful, yes, but it was something else too, and afternoons had been spent this way, wanting to turn it off, but not doing so. He saw the *banderillas* being placed.

This was the fight's second act, the harpoon-like instruments attaching to muscle and skin, in preparation for the matador's return to the fray. The four banderilleros slipped back toward the ring's circumference.

It was exactly five in the afternoon. Frank wiped sweat from his brow. The matador aimed the estoque, and killed quickly with skill. Frank changed the channel. An attractive airhead was chairing a gaudy discussion on something or other on Antenna 3, and his mind began to creep towards a state of impurity.

He got up and stretched. There was an ant colony on the floor. Someone shouted downstairs, but it sounded more joyful than anything. Frank found it comforting. He wiped nutshell fragments off the table with his hand, and went to the bedroom and threw them out the window. The ancient hag directly opposite eyed him malevolently.

He paced the flat in impatience. More ants were appearing. They were creeping down walls and marching across the floors. He swept at some with his hand. He sat down and drank a beer, feeling restless and hot. He flicked back to the bullfights.

Someone was calling outside. "Frank, Frank!" He went to the window and it was Sjal. His flat had no buzzer, and this was how people had to attract attention. It wasn't abnormal here, and he did the same when he went to hers.

She came up and sat down, and he got her water. She drank and breathed heavily. She was looking forward to her friends coming, and she wanted him to call round later, so he'd be there when she returned from work. He said that's what he was doing. They drank water together in the living room, and she spoke of a flamenco course she was taking. She'd been learning this dance for years. He listened to her rhythm descriptions, her talk of clapping and songs.

"Do you have a lot of ants or something?"

"Yes, I have a lot of ants or something."

She studied them creeping around her shoe.

"Where did you live in Paris?" he asked her. He wasn't familiar with the names of any areas, but he wanted to know.

"In the Marais. Do you know Paris?"

"No."

"Well it's on the Right Bank, beside the Centre Pompidou."

"The what?"

"The Centre Pompidou. What would you say, the Pompidou Centre? It's this big place with a library, and space for expositions or, yes, exhibitions sorry, and behind it there are people playing guitar and sitting down, and some people selling drugs and things as well. I studied in the library, and I knew a guy who used to write a book there. He was Irish too."

"What was it about?"

"The book? I have no idea. It took place in many cities."

They finished their water and sat. Frank moved and the couch groaned, the hot leather catching his skin. It was like molten velcro. Sjal had to leave, and did, and he sat there alone in the ant flat, thinking and twitching until ten rolled around.


He left at ten-thirty. He walked down calle Feria in the moonlight, some streetlights working, others emitting nothing at all. He had a plastic bag, litre beer bottles within. There was the clink of the glass, and the rustle of the plastic.

Beth opened the door.

"Where were you?" she said. "They cooked for us and everything."

He said he was sorry and scratched his head, and she laughed and told him Sjal's father was there too. "Thank God you brought beer, we're all out."

They ascended through the house and came to the roof. Frank stepped onto the tile and took in the table, the pasta, a new girl on each side of the table, Pernilla, and a tall white-haired gent of maybe sixty. Two stools remained. One was pushed back a little, and this must have been Beth's place, dislodged when she went to open the door. He sat in the other. He was introduced to Mette, a pretty blonde, Sjal's father, who smiled warmly, and Lise, who was beside him to his right.

He looked at her, said
hello, looked away, and turned back in astonishment.

In songs or sweet poetics, the stars would have come
crashing down. He gazed intently at her face. She was bouncing
her foot under the table, and her brown hair was tickling her
shoulders. She had a glass of red wine.
"So I hear you work in a hotel," said Sjal's father, and Frank was
brought back to the table, looking around and saying, "yes, just
in the mornings."

Sjal's father was a poet. He appeared to study everything
carefully, but in a vaguely amused and wondrous way, and Frank
could easily see him as a poet of the ordinary, instilling it
through words with a mystical import.
"I myself have worked in hotels," he said. "It was in one of them
that I found this shirt." He touched the fabric of his white shirt,
and Frank smiled in surprise. There was nothing distinctive
about the shirt at all.
"There is something interesting about the coming and going of
strangers, isn't there?"

Frank agreed with this, and laughed and said there was, and
he opened a bottle of beer and poured for those who wanted.
Beth moved plates to make more room. The night was pleasant,
and ended with Frank taking Lise and Mette to play pool. Mette
dozed in the corner of the hall.

Frank watched Lise shoot. She laughed and touched against
him, but she wanted to win too, and he was impressed and
intrigued by all she seemed to be. Maybe it's hard to know much
at first, but everything in life suggests that sometimes it is not.
She seemed to have such hard-won knowledge, yet be capable
of staggering, gorgeous warmth.

She was competitive but compassionate, wise but full of hope.
He took a shot, potted and took another, and she encouraged and
smiled. His eyes were going crazy, trying to see her and the ball
at once.

Walking home, the three of them spoke of travel – of places they had been, and places they wanted to go. Frank mentioned Berlin and Chicago. They had been to Berlin themselves, briefly, but were curious to hear of Chicago, and he embellished and spun the truth, for the purpose of making a story. They reached Sjal's door, and the girls hugged him goodnight.

The next evening there was a party. It was for something or other, in Sjal and Dev's house, and when Frank got there it was eleven o'clock, and full of people. He glanced around for Lise and saw her talking with a Spaniard. Dev ushered Frank away with the promise of whiskey, and started shouting about a Pogues cd he'd got for nothing in a flea-market. They sat in a corner and drank, various accents milling around.
"None of my fucking workmates turned up," complained Dev, laughing and shaking his head. "Stupid bastards."
A Dutch musician called Michael wandered over. "Hey, there's an old guy here," he said. From the expression on his face, maybe William of Orange was there, and Frank scanned the rooftop laughing, knowing full well it was Sjal's father. He spied him speaking earnestly with Beth.
"You'd better watch your bird!" Frank bellowed at Dev, and Dev got all animated and hyper, pretending he was going to roll up his sleeves and settle the Swedish poet. He emptied his glass and groaned loudly.

Frank went to the toilet but there was someone in there, so he waited in the hallway, comically clutching his bladder. The door opened and it was Lise.
"You're killing me," he shouted. "I'm dying."
She smiled and rubbed his arm. "Why am I killing you?"
"Because my body's going to explode, and you're talking to s ome guy."
She tilted her head sweetly. "We were just talking Frank."

His kidneys were screaming, but he didn't want to move. She said she'd wait. When they went back to the roof they sat together, her beautiful legs touching his, and he poured her Spanish wine while the party lurched and shook.
"I'm gonna go to bed soon," she whispered.
"Well I'm gonna walk you down."

In her room she closed the door. It was dark and warm and perfect, and they sat down on the bed and embraced. They held each other tightly and spoke nothing but the truth, and he thought this is what the world is when all your cards come up. It was as wonderful as that.

*He loves the sound of birdsong. The gentle morning chirp, all fresh and free of chains. He stands by his window just to hear it. These birds inhabit the trees around him, the trees planted on the street below, reaching to Allah. He smokes amid early birdcalls.*

*It's another sunny day in the capital. He eats bread and wants for nothing, lost in his future dream. Holy smoke, rolling. A dark blue bird alights on the ledge, head darting about, furtively. He stands motionless to observe.*

*The bird struts and stretches, occasionally moving its wings, but seemingly content here. It pecks at the chipped white paint. For a second it loses its footing, recovers, and then continues as if nothing had happened. It is not scared misfortune will strike again.*

*He waves his hand and it's gone. Its muscles cut the air, and the wing motion sounds like a paper bag, filled by a gust of wind. The blue bird disappears. In the sunshine morning he is once again alone, framed in his window for anyone looking up.*

*It's all about generating the right heat to twist metal. Then the building will collapse into itself. This was made to work before, by others, in America. He had watched in fascination. He had felt then part of something huge and humble, this holy vengeance, although he knew not the perpetrators, nor their plan. This was what was so awing. There were others out there, with similar aims, and clearly this was no coincidence. There were forces at work. Action had been commanded. He was merely a cog in a waking machine, a chosen instrument, and he would do what he would do, without fear. The time was drawing near.*

*He lights a cigarette, and exhales. More birds circle about. His gums bleed nearly every day, red droplets splashing into the sink. He ignores it. In its way it is purification, bloodletting, and he stares at the red lines. The trickles. It's a small and sharp reminder.*

*Spill your own to take from others. Show you have no fear. Whatever is requested you must do. This must be understood.*

*Back home he had killed for belief. Soon he will do the same. The French will pay, the West will pay, Christianity will suffer as it made others do. He knows the building to hit. Sparks and rubble, and a haughty tower reduced to dust. Plans and explosives. He stands by the window smoking a cigarette, and he can see it all before him, like the mending of a wound.*

*He hears children below. He is returned to his surroundings. The sun hits his face, the smoke curls away, and he smiles for an instant, alone. Birds flying and chirping. The everyday and ordinary, his external life, floats around his body. Moments waft like smoke. He stands in the morning in the city of Beirut, a city once known as the Paris of the Middle East.*

# CAUSALITY

The car pushed through the world, in darkness. The girls were happily drunk, talking and laughing in the back seat. Aria knew she was going to get hiccups. The taxi flashed down the Right Bank Expressway, and she craned her neck around to see the Eiffel Tower. At night it gave her goose bumps.

It was April. The car ascended, and began moving northeast towards Republique. Aria fumbled for the fare, not wishing to delay the man when they got there. They were dropped at l'Hopital Saint Louis, and walked home in two minutes. Laura started making toast.
"Do we have any of that wine left?" she asked over her shoulder, scanning the fridge for butter. Aria saw a half bottle on the counter.
"Yeah, there's lots."
They drank and ate, the light flickering softly, the bulb nearly gone. It was cooler now than in February, especially at night. March had been fine, and now April had taken this little dip. Presumably it was temporary. Aria worked in a café selling Swedish bread, American cookies, and overpriced French supermarket soup. Very rarely did she misunderstand an order, and Laura was amazed by this. Two months is not long she told her, when you're trying to learn a language.

Laura always said it was to Aria's advantage that she'd never done a French course, but Aria wasn't sure. Whether it was true or not, not a day went by without Laura cursing her Sorbonne study. "Je deteste la grammaire," she'd shout, screeching and laughing at once. The windows would shake when she did.

They had jam, butter, wine and bread. They spilt crumbs everywhere. Aria loved this French wine, its simple, correct taste. Red wine in the evenings was lovely.

They heard a noise from outside. There was this guy who kept coming around, shouting obscenities about American girls. They heard the sound of a trash can being kicked, and knew it was him. He called out now about American foreign policy, and the treatment deserved by degraded American girls.

He cursed and swore. Aria hated this, much more than Laura did, and she was terrified to even look out the window. It made her feel sick.

After a while he left. It was probably only five minutes, but it felt longer. Aria rolled her shoulders. Laura peered out to check he was really gone. It was bad enough having strange, silent men eye her malevolently on the metro, without feeling trapped in her own home. They drank some more without speaking.

The evening had been fun; out in a few bars, exchanging a few glances. They tried to dwell on this part. The toast was only half-eaten, and it was cold now, and Aria felt sad and ashamed just looking at it. This guy dug up her past for her unwanted, and the fact he didn't know what he was doing was slim consolation. She felt small and unsure.

Soon after they went to bed. Someone was revving an engine, again and again, and Aria lay in silence, listening. She pulled the blankets tighter, and thought of her mother and sister. Two months was the longest she'd ever been away, and a little sentimentality can be excused now and then. She cried softly, and felt warmer.

Frank lay in bed. He didn't want to get up today, but he knew he'd have to eventually. Hunger and thirst would prevail. He could hear rain outside, the swish of passing cars, and he curled foetus-like into himself. The room was dark, a gloomy anytime darkness, but he felt it was around midday, and was depressed by this fact alone.

He remembered the moment of impact. It just came to him, and he flinched and tightened. His breathing and heart rate increased. He lay on his back with his jaw like a bear trap, clenched and protruding to the point of pain. The room swam momentarily.

He got up and made breakfast. He didn't want to shower or sleep. He ate quickly, anxiously, and didn't bother washing up. Then he changed his mind and did. He suddenly had to leave the flat, and rushed about, dressing, grabbing keys, and checking he really had done the dishes. He cracked his hip off a chair and cried out. He made sure the oven was off, checked the water in the toilet wasn't still running, and scrambled out the door. On the rainy street he relaxed.

He slowed his pace and walked northward. He passed the metro station for Porte de Vanves, right next to his flat, on the southern edge of the city.

"Rather the rain than a train," he said aloud, feeling better now, and smiling at the stupidity of it. "Rather the rain than a train."

He turned right, went down Boulevard Brune, and took a left onto rue Didot, again heading north. This street was calming for some reason. He slowed further, and felt happy now, his hands warm, despite the cold rain. He smiled, feeling genuine relief. Three workmen were gathered around a truck, and, as he passed, one of them accidentally knocked against him and excused himself. Frank felt a beautiful tickle somewhere in his head, comforted by the contact.

He walked on, feeling light and almost crying, squeezing his fists in sheer unbridled joy. He came onto bustling Avenue du Maine, and up ahead was la Tour Montparnasse. A Parisian skyscraper. There were lights on inside, piercing in the midday gloom.

Newspaper shops stuffed with pornography were scattered around and about. He entered none. He came to the beginning of rue de Rennes, leading straight and true to Saint Germain-des-Pres. He bought some roasted chestnuts, but the idea was more interesting than the taste.

Halfway along rue de Rennes his ankle gave him trouble. He stopped, grimacing. He leaned against a bus stop and eased it gently back and forth, hoping to click it free again. This sometimes took time. A few passers-by were looking, but he was used to this. It popped free, and he gasped in sudden pain.

He continued north gingerly, and it loosened further. The cold and rain never helped. He was shivering now, drops falling from his nose, and the cold and congestion were dampening his spirits. Car horns and shopping bags. A dog pissed against a bank machine, a security guard eyeing it with distaste.

Frank reached the Seine, and sheltered under Pont Neuf. There was something beautiful in standing under a bridge in the rain, despite the fact he was cold, soaking, and there wasn't even anywhere to sit. The river was misty, and had risen slightly. A cruiser went by, empty save for a few downstairs, and one lunatic braving the elements on deck. Foamy waves rolled outward. Frank rubbed his hands vigorously, and sang softly to himself.

Johnny ignored the hookers. He was on rue Saint-Denis, in the evening time. He was eating a crepe and waiting for that fool Michel, who owed him money as usual. He saw him come out of some place further up, whistled, and when Michel arrived they strolled back to Beaubourg. Johnny didn't really feel angry about the money, but he still wasn't leaving without it.

They sat down and drank. Johnny huddled inside his leather coat, and Michel looked at it enviously. He'd come from his audition wearing only a shirt. The crowd thinned out before their eyes, night coming down, and the tourist bellies rumbling. Johnny spat champagne on the ground.

Michel handed over the cash. He didn't even have to be asked. Johnny counted it carefully, but felt ridiculous doing so, as no resistance had been offered. He stuck it in his pocket.

"I want to improve my English," said Michel, in English.
"Tu parles anglais?" said Johnny, surprised. He looked at him with interest.
"Un peu, mais je veux parler bien."
There was silence after this. Johnny didn't know what was coming next.
"Est ce que…" faltered Michel, stopping.
"Oui?" said Johnny, guessing now. "Qu'est ce que c'est?"
"Est ce que, uh, on peut parler anglais un peu?" stammered Michel, scratching furiously at his right eyebrow.
"Maintenant?"
"Ouais, si tu veux."
Johnny roared with laughter.
Si je veux?" he coughed, wiping his chin. "C'est toi, putain. Qu'est ce que tu veux French boy?"
"Moi je veux parler anglais," said Michel.
"What is your name?" said Johnny. "How old are you? Tell me."
"Arret," said Michel.
"Quoi," shouted Johnny, in hysterics now. "Tu veux parler anglais ou non? What is your fucking name?"
"Michel," said Michel.
"What?"

"My name is Michel."

"Very good. How old are you?"

Michel grimaced. "I am 29 years old."

"And what do you like to do?" asked Johnny, falling over on his side. He was enjoying this, but he didn't want Michel to know it. The prospect of English conversation sounded good for some reason.

"I like to read and spend the time with my girlfriend."

"Spend time."

"Pardon?"

"Spend time, not the time."

"Oh, OK, and spend time with my girlfriend."

"Very good," said Johnny, approvingly.

He lit a cigarette, then reached back in his pocket and gave another to Michel. He blew out smoke, cheeks puffed, and Michel flicked the lighter for a flame. They continued.

"Tell me all the different types of weather you can have in English."

"In English or in England?"

"In English and in England," said Johnny, although he hadn't meant that at all. "Tell me 'bout that London fucking weather."

"Well," said Michel. "It can do snow…"

"What?"

"It can do snow, rain…"

"No it can't."

"Yes, I think that it can. The cold. Like here you know."

Johnny sucked the smoke.

"Don't say that. It can snow, it can rain, it can…I don't know, be cloudy."

"It can be cloudy," said Michel.

They drank some more in silence. Johnny surveyed the deserted square, or, as he came to notice now, the near-deserted square. There was a figure moving slowly across, down by the Pompidou entrance. He squinted in the darkness, trying to make out who it was, wondering if maybe he knew him. Smoke rose skyward.

Whoever it was changed course, climbing the sloping square diagonally. This brought him gradually nearer as he passed. His jacket was ripped and threadbare, his chin hunched toward his chest. His feet seemed to shuffle more than step. Johnny stared, still unsure if he'd ever seen him before. He pursed his lips and sniffed.

"You look at him," said Michel. It is who?"

"Je ne sais pas. Personne."

"Il n'est pas Francais. Anglais, peut-etre."

The figure drank from a can. He put it back in his pocket and shuffled on, leaving the square and disappearing down a side street. Johnny and Michel were alone.

"Il n'etait pas Francais," repeated Michel. "Anglais, peut-etre."

"Ouais, peut-etre."

Michel took out a notebook and scribbled phrases down. Johnny saw him write 'it can be snowy,' but said nothing. He was tired now.

Yes he had seen that guy before, somewhere, but he didn't know him, he was sure of that. Someone else uncertain of the place they had been set. That's all. He stood up and stretched and yawned.

"It can be very fucking cold," said Michel.

The lights were on in the Centre, the empty library brighter than day. Blue and red pipes snaked upwards. An enormous picture of some dead personage flapped in the wind, an artist being exhibited Johnny presumed.

He'd been in the Centre Pompidou many times, but he'd only ever wandered around the free sections.

Michel stood up too, and Johnny punched him in the stomach. He had energy to unleash. It wasn't hard enough to hurt, but maybe to hurt a little, and Michel groaned in shock for a moment, before swinging deftly back. They flailed at each other in mock viciousness, observed unawares by a table-stacking waiter, who'd seen all this before, many times. Johnny seized Michel in a headlock.

"It can be snowy, French boy," he shouted, laughing and hitting at the same time.

He rubbed the top of Michel's head with his fist, a knuckleduster. Michel hissed, and Johnny stopped and released. They swayed in the moonlight, regaining breath.

"Je ne peux pas dire, 'it can be snowy'?" gasped Michel, coughing.

"C'est pas grave," Johnny snorted. "Tu peux le dire si tu veux."

Karen dreamed in colour. She woke up and tried to remember, but couldn't recall any images. Just colour. She got the bus to the office and fielded calls – handling enquiries, patching people through, talking to clients from Boston to Bordeaux. She liked the feeling of the swivel chair.

For lunch they went to a local café. It was just Karen and Claire, a workmate and a friend, and they ate and talked of Julie, who'd gone to Amsterdam. The waitress messed up the order.

Back on the street they walked in silence, digesting, taking a moment before work re-commenced. Karen never minded walking alone, but it was better with two. A pair of eyes at hand. They crossed the road and took a right.

"Maybe we should take another way," said Claire, "there seems to be some kind of demonstration up ahead."

They turned and retraced steps. Karen loved Claire's London accent, possessing as it did a delicacy she felt hers lacked. She was sometimes conscious of being an American, in light of the roiling world.

"What did it look like they were protesting?" she asked.

"Non a la guerre."

"That stupid fucking war."


The rest of the day went by in a blur. The feel of the office was one of random chaos. Later that night she remembered pausing once to drink some water, and in her memory, that moment seemed to take place in total silence. All the bustle and din temporarily ceased, and she was separate and detached, magnificently.

It's funny how time can do this she thought, create aching perfection from seconds long past. We slow down, speed up, alter unconsciously shaping events, and all to make things function, a life as a narrative. Karen in midday silence. When the water touched her tongue, it was like she could remember every other single time it had done so, clearly and distinctly. From birth and maybe before. It was remembering so as to forget.

Today Claire had told of how she'd miscarried aged 21. Seven years in the past. Karen had listened in sadness and shock, wishing then she could see her face in that café, and not merely touch her tears across a table. Claire had never told anyone before. There isn't much to say with true pain, the loss of a child that was never a child. There isn't much to say or to do.

"Non a la guerre! George Bush non!" The chants and screams of peace, another little memory.

Aria went to the graveyard. Laura was studying, so she walked there alone, a grey-cloud sky impassive overhead. It was a twenty minute walk, heading eastward.

Pere Lachaise cemetery is a city of the illustrious dead. Maps are easily available, celebrity locations highlighted in red. On its leafy, peaceful walkways, she felt detached nonetheless.

She was looking for Jim Morrison, and was excited to be doing so. A curious, simple moment awaited. She followed curling pathways, the map held at her side, sweet anticipation for something so mundane. The headstone of a famous man, the inscription.

Frank stood, reading. On the back of Oscar Wilde's tomb lay a quotation from The Ballad of Reading Gaol, a paean to Oscar's separate status, and the sorrowful life of the outcast. Frank smiled in compassion.

He had never made the trip to Pere Lachaise before, and had often wanted to. Today was as good as any. A dirt-grey sky, a rain-threat. He felt safe in the company of Oscar.

Frank had never really cared about The Doors, but maybe it would be interesting to visit Jim Morrison's grave as well. His final resting place, after a lurid, bloated life.

Aria stood in wonder. This was fascinating, the simple, unadorned headstone, just James Douglas Morrison – no graffiti, nothing. A guard hovered nearby, making sure it stayed that way. Someone had placed a feather and an arrow on the ground. There were a few tourists circling, and then a young, scruffy guy arrived on the scene. His body language was uncertain, ill at ease.

He looked to be in his mid-twenties – tall and thin, but really not her type. She turned away. Now he was looking at her. She flicked her hair and swallowed, not feeling uncomfortable, just standing still. Yes, he was watching her all right.

The guard's radio crackled alive, and she flinched for a moment, and her eyes met this stranger's, briefly. She saw his flickering pain.

Frank gazed at this beautiful girl, her long hair and gentle dark eyes, and thought himself desperately ugly, and blinked. His head lowered, and he coughed.

Aria smiled in kindness, but he didn't see this, and then he turned his back and walked away. It was all too much to believe there were girls like this right now. If he was never going to touch what he held in his dreams, it was best not to fall into such reverie. Things just happen, eyes meet.

Frank left the graveyard, and descended to the metro station. He jumped the barrier after an old man, kicking the gate to pass freely through. When the train came he boarded quickly, his stomach rumbling, his nose cold. The carriage rattled steadily.

Back on the surface, Aria wandered round.
She passed writers, artists, and whole families with German names, all buried equally, in the soft tended earth. She paused in thought on a bench.

Johnny felt the lessons were going well. Michel had made significant advances, and he was now attempting to teach him the conditional.

"It's all about possibility," he kept shouting. "If I found some money, I would keep it."

"It's all about possibility," said Michel. "If I found some money, I would keep it."

"Exactly," said Johnny. "The possibility of 'if.'"

It was sunny by the Centre Pompidou. Johnny broke off the lesson momentarily to rattle out a bloodcurdling folk song of anger and death. An elderly couple vacated the area.

"Wishes and maybes," said Johnny, putting down the guitar. "All the wishes and maybes, of the world."

"What might happen," ventured Michel, timidly.

"Ouais," said Johnny, leaping up, "c'est ca. What might happen. It's the same thing."

Michel scribbled something in his notebook.

"You can just translate," Johnny explained, sitting back down and snorting. "If I would I could. You know?"

"Yes."

They let this knowledge permeate. Johnny's teaching fire was going out for today, and he leaned back and reached for a smoke. Michel did the same. The familiarity of the scene was comforting. The people were different, but everyday it was basically the same. The international throng, taking a break from their lives. Johnny in his leather, the guitar so old and worn.

"So do you think I am learning well?"

"I don't know. Do you?"

"I think I am doing OK."

"Then there's no need to ask me."

"No, not really. There is not."

"I think that's OK for today."

Johnny scanned the piazza, establishing who was where. There was that Chinese busker doing U2 songs – his competition, his nemesis. One love, not the same, got to cally each other, cally each other…The guy was hopeless, but passionate.

Johnny stood up to stretch again, and his phone rang as his body loosened, the beeping signal cutting short his cat-like extensions. He snapped it from his pocket and listened. "Je ne peux pas," he said, and hung up. He sat back down, clicking his fingers.

For the rest of the day he sang songs and drank. Michel left and others arrived, and it was always like this in the springtime. There were jokes and stories, and strange little moments that caught him unawares. Once a child came over and hugged him. A juggler performed to his left, with bowling pins and then with fire. Johnny sat and watched, a tiredness now descending.

Aria was at work. Customers came and went – coffee, bagels and currency, blurrily changing hands. She sighed and wiped her brow. It was another two hours before she finished, and she was feeling stressed today, being the only one on the till. Someone was looking for banana bread.

She explained it was gone and he didn't understand, and she had to explain again, feeling stupid and pretty pissed.
"It is gone?" he said in faltering English, like they always did when they wouldn't listen to her French. "Yes," she said. "That's what I already told you."

The owner came in and observed her, hawk-like, from a distance. She was paranoid about staff giving so much as a cookie to a friend. She hovered in a corner, fingers clicking, and pursed her mouth. Aria tried to ignore her.

The smell of the bagels was sick-sweet. In the beginning, she had loved their taste and smell, but now they made her queasy, and she never took one herself. Still, the job was fine, and if it didn't feel that way today, at least she was aware this was an exception. She tied back her hair during a free moment.
"Hey," said Laura, brandishing a student paper. She'd just walked in off the street. The owner visibly stiffened, Aria noticing out of the corner of her eye. She contemplated giving Laura a whole pack of cookies, and giggled in her mind. Laura had made page six of the paper.
"Look," she said. "It's that thing I wrote about Lorca. I really didn't think they'd print it."
Aria wanted to read it, but she couldn't right then. A guy wanted to pay for a cappuccino, and she clanged open the cash register and deposited the change. The owner left abruptly.
"Read it to me," said Aria. "I want to hear it, but I just can't read right now. Go on, there aren't too many customers."
"OK," said Laura. "It's not too long anyway."
She folded the paper and cleared her throat. Aria laughed, and Laura started reading.

*"Garcia Lorca and the Children Still Unborn,"* she declared,
*"by Laura Taylor."*

*"'We walk on*
*an unsilvered*
*mirror,*
*a crystal surface*
*without clouds.*
*If lilies would grow*
*backwards,*
*if roses would grow*
*backwards,*
*if all those roots*
*could see the stars*
*and the dead not close*
*their eyes,*
*we would become like swans.'*

*"Earth" by Federico Garcia Lorca*

"Lorca was…" Laura began, and then the owner cut her short.
"I don't pay you for this," she said in English. Aria coughed and
apologised, and Laura stepped back in surprise. Neither of them
had seen her re-enter. Aria messed with her hair, and Laura
moved towards the doorway. The owner exhaled dramatically.

There were no customers to deal with in that moment, so
Aria was forced to busy herself doing nothing, while she was
silently rebuked. It was a long moment. She heard a car horn
from outside, and the yell of some irate pedestrian. A DJ yapped
on the radio.

Eventually the owner left again, skulking away like a
creature of the night. Aria relaxed, and rolled her shoulders. She
felt like a scolded schoolgirl, and fiddled with a sugar packet as
a distraction. Nobody in the café now. Very soon this day would
be over, or at least this part of it.

The sun spread out on the tile floor, revealing dirt patches she thought she'd cleaned. She turned off the radio. The bagel smell wafted round her, and all the other smells and sounds. The coffee, the coffee machine. She looked at the mop in the corner, at the tea towel on the counter. "As long as there are people, there'll be sun and death and rain," said a sign on the wall. Aria yawned in boredom.

A woman came in and ordered soup, and so it was Aria and this woman together alone, the server and the served, like a woodcarving or a sketch. Supermarket soup, at a price to make her blush.

"Oh, c'est delicieuse," exclaimed the woman, beaming.
Aria thanked her and smiled.
"C'est vraiment delicieuse," the woman repeated, the type of woman who would never buy supermarket soup.

Aria went back behind the counter, and asked her if she wanted the radio on. She didn't, and the silence was sweet. They each went about their business in the afternoon, the woman eating, and Aria cleaning absently. She dusted and pottered about.

The clock wound on, and then she could finally close the shop. The metal shutters rolled down, and she was free for the day and happy. The sun hit her eyes and she passed down the street like a leaf.

She made a detour by the river, and leaned against the wall on Pont Neuf, watching the sparkling water. There were readers and strollers on the banks, and a tourist cruiser lay berthed to one side. A queue was forming for the next sailing, and she wondered what it was like to see the city in this way, and whether any queuing tourists would mistake her for a native. Une vraie Parisienne.

She started heading home, cutting across the square at the back of the Pompidou Centre, down rue Rambuteau, and up rue du Temple, to Place de la Republique. It was about a twenty minute walk, all in all. She felt that big-city lull and comfort – a peace in the eye of the storm sensation. Millions of dreams and thoughts, all around.

She crossed over Republique, and took the back streets to the canal. Here she paused again on one of the hump-back bridges – slow, placid water, perfect underneath. Two old men were fishing to her right, and a guy working in a video shop over the other side had stepped out for a smoke. The water caught the setting sunlight.

As she reached l'Hopital Saint Louis, she turned her head to the left, and a jutting piece of the Sacre Coeur shone between the buildings. It was illuminated already, though the sun had not completely sunk. Aria rounded the corner and the view disappeared, and now she was on her street, with the old and battered cobblestones. She would be home in less than a minute, and was dying to read Laura's piece.

Frank had been losing all morning. He began to suspect maybe the deck held only fifty-one, but when he counted, they were all present and correct. The day passed in this manner, and when evening came he had not eaten very much.

He went to the kitchen and rummaged. Bread, crisps, some fruit juice. A banana he didn't feel like. He gathered them up and returned to the living room, sitting on the floor and eating slowly.

The crisps were stale, but he ate them anyway, and was glad of them. The bread was in a similar state. He returned to playing solitaire and trying not to think of that girl from the graveyard. He was losing at both. The game kept grinding to a halt before he could complete it, and his mind kept making pictures of her eyes locking with his. He sighed and rubbed his face, stretching the skin on his cheeks. He blinked and gave a cough.

He turned his cards and they presented no options. He shuffled and re-dealt. A red jack, a black six, and other uninspiring selections. He ran through the remaining deck, made a few moves, did so again, and there was nothing else. He shuffled and re-dealt.

What had she made him think of, that dark-haired graveyard girl? What did he feel he had shown? He yawned and scanned the cards. Abandoning the game, he closed his eyes and tried to relive the scene. He sat quietly, but then saw a flash of the accident. There was a sharp pain in his left arm, like a violent twisting. His eyes snapped open, and he rose to his feet, hands twitching. He blundered into the kitchen.

He ran the tap and drank some water. He wanted to leave but didn't. If the mere act of going outside could make him feel better, than surely there was nothing really wrong. He smiled faintly at this. He heard somebody closing a window, his neighbour down below, and was warmed and quietened slightly. He stretched and felt some trembling.

The trembling always pleased him. It happened once in a while, a soft and warming shake, and he felt so new and whole then temporarily. He had come to wondering if there was a way to make it start. He drank a little more water.

He sat down, felt stillness for a moment, and then his mind clouded with memories of Lise, and Sjal, and Monica. He was breathing through his nostrils. He was unsure how necessary it was to remember these people now, these places. How much good was it serving? He was twenty three, and already familiar with so many streets and faces, fleetingly. Did he put too much weight on encounters?

Leaning back, he felt his stomach gurgle, and a strange and calming sensation slide slowly within. It was like a glacier dissolving, an ice-rock of energy, thawing. He coughed and resisted an urge to move. His body buckled suddenly, into itself, and his mind was on that Berlin bus. The crash and the smash. He waited for it to pass. It did in time, and his thought returned to Lise. He relaxed.

All those nagging memories, of Sevilla and before. Maybe it was time to start saying goodbye.

His reference point was the last one. When he thought of a take, he could only remember the last one. The girl right there beneath him. He turned over, propping himself up on his elbow. He was lying on the bed, fully clothed.

Before he left his mother had called him over. He'd been frightened, in a rush. She had whispered in his ear. Some things never grant an ending, they just gradually fall away. These men have given you one. This country is not yours now, and you are truly free. He had slunk out the back door.

Johnny tugged on the hair at the back of his head. His breath prevented silence. He lay still, scrunching up his face and closing his eyes. You are truly free.

They kicked him from Dakar for reasons he had buried. He wound his way to Paris. Jean, Johnny, whatever. He was lying on the bed, propped up on his elbow. His reference point was the last one.

He hated memory with all his heart. Girls, places, feelings. He strove constantly to forget, to deny, to wrestle the past right out of his head. He had learned the hard way how this only made things worse. In the course of an average day, remembrances would surface, and the more he pushed them back, the more they buried in.

He had not returned to the place of his birth for over three years. He had reached a wounded acceptance this would last forever. Would become ten years, twenty, death. He remembered learning English and French in the local school as a child. He sat up on the bed, those kids down below, playing football.

He drank water. He wanted to drink water today. He tuned his guitar. The strings strained and tightened, pleading with him to be replaced. He couldn't be bothered getting new ones. He started a song but abandoned it halfway through. He threw the thing on the bed.

He thought about calling someone, but he would be called sooner or later. Maybe he'd go to Beaubourg. Michel would probably turn up for an English lesson.

He had not seemed to notice that Johnny was losing heart. He'd taken to arriving with print-outs from the internet, rolling reams of grammar he was all hyped up to learn. Johnny had no idea what a 'question tag' might be.

The guitar fell off the bed. It banged below, and he eyed it with disdain. He picked it up and tuned it again, squeaking round the pegs till they finally did his bidding. Somebody shouted something outside, and although he didn't hear what, he knew it was for him. He flung the key out the window, so whoever it was could come up.

A slovenly character appeared, claiming he'd managed to dig up money from somewhere. Johnny stared at him, as he emptied notes and coins onto the bed. How much was there he wanted to know.

The cokehead shuffled, sniffling and mumbling while his fingers clicked a rhythm. Johnny gave him his money's worth, and ushered him out the door.

He played a song and played another, loosening up. He stretched and cracked his knuckles. High beyond the rooftops, the clouds unleashed their load, and dirty heavy raindrops hit the turning world. Johnny was glad he'd stayed in today, because money must be made. He lit a cigarette.

Karen and Michel were walking. Michel described the scenery, in English, until she asked him not to. He held her hand instead. They were in Parc de la Villette on a Sunday afternoon.

"There are very huge trees," said Michel, unable to resist, and she squeezed his hand and he stopped. Someone rolled by on a bike.

Michel went to the bathroom and came back soon after, hyper and more alert. He rubbed and touched against her. "Relax," she said. "Today I want to relax."

They walked on slowly, and she could feel the strain as he tried to control his fidgeting. Sometimes she wondered whether…but always dismissed it as silly. She didn't know what she was talking about anyway. She could hear birdsong and distant voices, and then the sound of two bikes passing. A woman called out to a man.

Later they made love, and she stroked his hair as he lay breathing against her. His breath massaged her skin. His day's energy was spent, and nothing else remained now, save a promised sleep. She put her arms around him, shielding out the world.

"Your English is really good now sweetie. You've improved such a lot."

He murmured something inaudible. They had not made love in his apartment for some time. She relaxed into its feeling.

She knew he was asleep now, the breathing and the weight, and she let his body lie there, like a stone. Her legs were warm and tired.

Sometimes she worried about him. She knew he worried for her. Sometimes she wondered what his life was, and did she really know him at all. Other times she deemed this ridiculous – a banal conceit, applicable to anyone when in a certain mood. She sighed in warm contentment, her lover's skin her own.

His behaviour today in the park. Was today the first such occurrence of this, or maybe the fourth or fifth? Was this a part of their life, unnoticed until now?

She struggled to recollect. The change in his mood, the tension and speed. Was she aware of this always, unconsciously?

He coughed and was still once more. She squeezed close her eyes in defence. She must think uninterrupted. A foreboding something flicked through her body. Maybe she'd only created it, brought it on through worry, not discovered a dormant dread. His weight was strong on her chest now.

The tension and speed, the package she'd got. She didn't know what she was talking about anyway. She rested her cheek on his hair.

Michel woke up and they talked about nothing. She avoided all questions and doubt. He asked about use of the conditional, and she tried to remember herself.

Within an hour he was back asleep. On her breast as before. She slowly pushed him off her, turning on her side and curling inward. The warmth of the bedclothes spread. The conditional is "would"; yes, she'd said it right. Possibility.
Michel began to snore, a bee-like droning hum, and her shoulder now was tickled, by the push of his breath. He was sleeping, and she loved him.

He kept on sending letters. Aria was at the kitchen table, the clock at half past one, and she read through once more, slowly.

It was wrong. She could not continue this, though she knew he meant her well. It was all too long ago. Placing the letter down, she clasped her hands together, stretching. A page swept off the table.

He was a guy she'd met in LA. Visiting some friends there, in her 16 year old summer, she'd met this English DJ and told him all her thoughts. They'd held each other's hand. They'd written for a while, but then she changed her mind. Things became difficult in her life. Since she moved to Paris, he'd got back in touch.

This letter today was the sixth. The first had come in March, after a silence of two and a half years. It had been exciting, and she'd replied instantly. Told him all her news. He knew nothing of the trauma, the pictures or the pain, and she mentioned none of it. And this was the problem.

She didn't know to talk to someone who didn't know her now. She guessed he must be twenty three. Did he not understand this? She had stopped writing after the third letter. It just seemed better that way. She picked the fallen page up, and placed the whole thing back in its envelope. She smoothed the tiny creases.

Today was easy sunshine. It was the middle of June, the 18th. She poured a glass of water. She leaned out the window and looked at the trash cans, spilling a few drops of water below. Today she was free from work.

She went for a walk by the canal. She watched the rippling water. A Twix wrapper struggled for life, ducking under and re-emerging, and Aria on the bank smelt smoke from a cigarette. She stopped and stood in silence.

This neighbourhood felt real to her, her flatmate and her flat. The bakery, the streets. Rue Bichat, rue Alibert, rue Saint Maur. A taxi motored past. She sat down by the water, and trailed her finger in the flow.

Why was he writing now? Should she be scared or not? She felt probably not. She flicked her wet hand, and water splashed on the concrete. It made a peculiar design. It might have been a troll's face. She made another pattern alongside it.

Later she went to the movies. It was enjoyable how so many in Paris went alone. All those small cinemas, no popcorn, no lights, and she sat comfortably with strangers, happy in the dark. She was mid-way down, sharing the space with six others.

It was a Spanish movie. Hable con Ella. Parle avec Elle. Talk to Her. Aria watched with full concentration – crystal images, Spanish words, French subtitles. Music from hearts that were lonely. She tied back her hair.

The film was low and gentle, the kind she'd like to speak of with a stranger in an airport. The silence of a coma. She cried a little, with the music and the pulse. She smiled. There was a woman somewhere sniffling in the gloom, talking calmly to herself. It wasn't annoying at all.

Aria saw this film as being about belief. A belief some might find intolerable, perhaps. It was bubbling up with truth. When she left the cinema, which was just off rue Beaubourg, she walked over to the piazza and sat looking up at the Centre Pompidou. There were tourists all around.

She got up and left. Crossing rue Beaubourg, she entered le Marais, and strolled easily down rue Rambuteau. There was an old man selling strawberries. He shouted gruff obscenities at passers-by, insulting both his customers and those who ignored him.

She reached the intersection with rue du Temple. Turning left would have pointed her homeward, but she went straight through. The streets were clean here, the moneyed and tourists mixing freely. Catty men leaned from extortionate boutiques.

She was on rue des Francs Bourgeois. There was sunshine on the street. She walked its length, arriving at Boulevard Beaumarchais, and turning right onto Place de la Bastille. Over the far side, skaters were practising.

She reached the intersection with rue du Temple. Turning left would have pointed her homeward, but she went straight through. The streets were clean here, the moneyed and tourists mixing freely. Catty men leaned from extortionate boutiques.

She was on rue des Francs Bourgeois. There was sunshine on the street. She walked its length, arriving at Boulevard Beaumarchais, and turning right onto Place de la Bastille. Over the far side, skaters were practising.

A man laughed easily, sitting outside a smart looking café. His companion took his hand. She rolled it softly in hers, and Aria saw this in passing, all the tiny moments of the moving, living city. A dog inspected a lamp post.

She sat down for a while, and watched the skaters. This was all the boys ever did back home. They jumped and rolled and tripped and crashed, and there was padding, and a lingo. She was sure there was a French lingo too. She flicked a fly from her trainers.

Traffic kept obscuring her view. Whenever one of them completed a manoeuvre, he immediately engaged in a complicated handshake with all the others. White boys, with their slaps and chest thumps. They nodded and kept their cool, balancing and failing, and starting once again.

"You are American, I believe."

A man sat down beside her, lighting a cigarette.

She shifted, startled a little, this thick French accent taking her by surprise. Her body folded and curled.

"Tell me your name, American girl. Beautiful American girl."

She went to get up, but his hand touched her arm.

"Beautiful American girl."

She froze for a moment, but then turned to look at him full on. A smoker's face, searching eyes. He coughed twice, and she thought he must be in his forties, a sleepy rumble in his chest. His hand went to brush her hair.

She was walking quickly. She was conscious of nothing, just her movement on the street. Her muscles were tight.

She dodged pedestrians, rounded bends, kept her body streamlined as she cut through gaps and space. Eventually she began to slow, and finally stopped and shook.

The energy expelled, and she knew she was alright. She smiled in sweet relief. One thought came to her. She definitely wouldn't be writing to that guy from LA.

Frank began to tremble. He had been practising constantly for two and a half weeks, and every time he did it, he felt a little more. Shaking, warmth, expansion. He lay inert on his bed, fearless of this stillness where before it was too much. His feelings danced within him.

The physical sensations of his body were numerous and strange. They were everchanging. He felt lumps, gurgles, wires and spheres and spikes, all within the housing of his skin. His mind flashed random pictures.

Sometimes this healing lasted merely thirty seconds, others it stretched out to fifteen minutes or longer. He smiled or cried or both, a world within his chest. Pictures came of the accident, but also of Monica, of Lise, of half-remembered moments from his childhood long ago. He observed what he was feeling.

Afterwards he would rest or sleep. He went walking in the evenings. There was a bridge which led over the Boulevard Peripherique, from Porte de Vanves to the sleepy town of Malakoff, and he stood there as the sun set, watching transfixed. Gold and pink and purple.

He passed through neighbourhoods. There was that deeply stirring Parisian light, the peaceful sensation of the summer, the evening. Day's end. Malakoff was not Paris, it was more a town that could have been anywhere, and the parts of the city it bordered weren't so bustling or strong. Sometimes he sat down on benches.

In the mirror in the mornings, it almost looked like his muscles were growing stronger. This couldn't really be, or maybe it could. He would stand straight before himself, taking in this body which now felt like his own. It was stronger, warmer.

Showers were sensual dreams. Falling water hit his being, and he could direct his consciousness to focus on just a shoulder, or a leg. It could be all in that one moment. When sitting he would settle on his sleeves against his wrists, or his collar on his neck. Numerous sensations would follow. Frank was enchanted by the power that he held, the same energy that had caused anxiety, now rendering him fresh and new.

He kept practising. He sensed into himself constantly, remembering to do it again and again regardless of activity or location. Soon it was how he lived, with him always. He walked and felt his muscles, sat and followed his breath. Drinking, he was the liquid. Sunsets were not sunsets, but the only event in the stationary world. The same for the wind or a car horn.

He took that Spanish poem from his pocket and threw it away. It floated down peacefully over the Boulevard Peripherique. The wind caught it and didn't, and it glided easily for spells, before being fluttered, or whipped, or re-directed. Finally it attached to a speeding bumper. Frank began to cry, and distant neon signs blurred in his watery gaze. Banks or building societies.

He kept walking, breathing. Breaths became fuller as energy dispersed. Light was clearer, sounds were sharper, thoughts were strangely optimistic. What was broken he thought, only blooms in midnight.

Johnny was at Beaubourg. Michel had wrangled another lesson out of him, and was seated alongside, smoking.

"Both / both of, neither / neither of, either / either of," said Michel, brandishing a grammar book like a weapon. Johnny's heart sank. Michel turned to the appropriate lesson, flicking the pages earnestly. Johnny eyed him forlornly.

"So all of these words are for two things," said Michel. "Not much things."

"Many things."

"They are for many things?"

"No," spat Johnny. "You say 'many things,' not 'much.'"

"Ah, yes. Many things."

Michel paused for a moment.

"But they are not for many things," he ventured. His shoulders hunched.

Johnny stared at him coldly. His mouth opened as if to speak, but then Michel realised he wasn't going to, and instead confirmed it for himself.

"They are for two."

Thus the lesson began. Johnny sat there scowling and correcting, and Michel prodded, questioned, and sniffed. Johnny felt a buzz in his jacket every time he got a message. Michel was desperate to learn, and was trying really hard.

"Both of us went to the party," he read.

Nevertheless, Johnny couldn't be bothered. He didn't even feel angry, it was just an unnecessary drag. He started fiddling with his phone.

He stood up, and announced he was going for a walk. Told Michel to keep studying. He turned to his right and skirted the top of the piazza, disappearing down rue des Lombards and emerging at Chatelet. Bus 58 was parked on Saint-Denis.

It felt good to change location, even if it was only around the corner. He watched the skirts and suits. He thought of jumping on the 58, unsure really where it went, but what was the use. He'd have to come back eventually. A child dropped an ice-cream and roared loudly, and its mother negotiated it onto the bus.

The screams grew muffled within.

He scanned the faces for want of a distraction. Get lost in the appearance of others. There were furrowed brows, tourist smiles. His jacket buzzed again. He went and bought a crepe, asking for sugar and chocolate, and the man behind the counter needed convincing he was serious. He ate quickly.

He wandered into a café and drank a cup of coffee. He played X's and O's on a napkin. An old Arab man beside him whispered to himself, folding and unfolding a torn off page from a phonebook. Johnny cracked his knuckles.

He leaned with his chin in his palm, feeling his breath make contact with his skin. Warm jets covered his nails. So many people talked and hummed to themselves in this city, at once entirely present, and somewhere far away. He threw a glance at the waitress.

Back at Beaubourg, Michel displayed his knowledge. He seemed to be completely in control of this topic, and Johnny was tempted to ask why he needed a teacher at all. A pigeon pecked a panino.

"You don't need me for your teacher."

"Yes, I think that I do."

"You don't."

They sat in momentary silence.

The pigeon extracted a large lump of mozzarella and scampered off. Johnny kicked the remaining bread, putting some distant between himself and it. The Chinese busker wailed.

A girl called Severine sat down beside them. Johnny knew her in passing, and had once woken up in her flat. He tried to recall something else.

She told him he looked well, and that she'd been promoted. She was evidently pleased. He felt embarrassed and put upon, and didn't try to hide it. She left a short time after.

"That was who?"

"No one."

"OK."

Michel went to buy some alcohol.

As they sat drinking in the sunshine, Johnny watched two teenage girls in whispered conversation. Their body language was private, conspiratorial. He felt that they were separate, but still wanted to be seen. He caught a glimpse of bra strap.

Do women have that many secrets he thought, or just a worship of secrecy? He turned to Michel and flicked his ear, and Michel said 'both of the girls are pretty.' Johnny rolled his eyes. This was German beer they were drinking, or claimed to be.

They finished the bottles and started on others, content to be drinking in another easy day. They flicked the bottle tops. Johnny reached for the guitar, and absently picked a pattern. He put some tremolo on the B string. The teenage girls swivelled their heads, and seemed to agree it would be interesting to approach. They sat at a respectable distance.

Johnny continued picking. He murmured or hummed occasionally, with no desire to erupt into full-blown song. One of the girls began playing with her ponytail. "Jouez monsieur," said her companion. He gave her a sly-dog smile. "Jouez une chanson pour nous." Michel leaned back on his elbows.

The police arrived on the square, and they hid the beer. Michel spotted them over the far side and placed the guitar case on top of their stash. Johnny went on with his playing. The girls began to talk amongst themselves, quietly, discussing some hope or ambition, or maybe reciting a poem. There was a rhythm to their interplay. Michel kept an eye on les flics.

"So what do you want to hear?" said Johnny. They didn't understand. He repeated it in French, turning a tuning peg slowly, and when they told him anything he gave them a quizzical look. Hair flicking ensued.

So he played something, anything, and they seemed to be satisfied, or at least pretended they were. He almost offered them beer by mistake. They watched him with wisdom and wonder, or with something approaching those two.

They scrutinised. He stretched out his arms in the evening, yawned, and quietly scrutinised back. Michel had left.

"I'm going to tell you something," said Johnny, standing up and knowing they wouldn't understand.

"Businessmen are fuckers, and love is impossible."

*The sun rises in the east, and sets in the west. The west is the dying part of the earth. He is comforted by this thought. The west is full of poison, is ravaged by its lust, is slowly disappearing like an image from its screens. He's aiding an unstoppable process.*

*He moves away from the window. He flicks his cigarette. As it falls to the street below, the last smoke leaves his body and mixes with the air. The air and Lebanese sunshine. He eats some drying bread, and lights another smoke. Smoking is good for thinking.*

*Walking in the mornings gives him lightness in his head. Idle wandering in the quartier. There are streets he always returns to, streets he knows like his hands. He has circuits that he uses, routes planned in his head, and every single morning he can choose a different one.*

*Every day is similar, and this is how it is supposed to be. There are few deviations. Stones are in the same place each time he passes. The objects never change. Parked cars, registrations plates, sundry decorations in windows and on doors. People. He's ghost-like as he passes, shrouded by belief.*

*Sound commands his focus. The noise of traffic, voices, his own feet as he moves. Birdsong. He listens with attention, walks slowly, and sometimes rolls his fingers, like two spiders on his arms.*

*Djinn is always thinking of the work he'll carry out. Perfecting by modification. The plan bounces and rolls in his brain - becoming, changing, real. He holds it like a prayer. On the rooftop in the evenings he whispers what he'll do. What Allah will do through him.*

*The sun sets while he watches. Slowly, by degrees. Over time the roof-light changes, shadows falling, lengthening. Temperature goes down. He shivers, but stiffens his muscles to prevent it further. He's tense as night takes over.*

*The devil of the west, and the irredeemable wrongs. The
sacrilege. He broods on retribution, on the details of the plan.
He works and re-works the motions. All around the air is
cooling, and his body is a bowstring, holding off the chill.
The roof and he are welded.*

*He has right upon his shoulders. Purpose. He walks the
streets, watches the sun, smokes. It's all prologue. It's a training
ground, a readying, a filing down of matter not needed by his
soul. An unburdening. As he stands upon his rooftop, he can feel
within him the time drawing near. His eyes close.*

*There is a near imperceptible wind on his face. Like child's
breath. It massages his forehead and cheeks. He's motionless.
When the student is ready, the Master will appear. He's a statue
on the roof, awaiting divine instructions.*

*He's eating some bread made with raisins. He's smoking his last
cigarette. The birds are still singing, the apartment's been sold.
He's looking at ways of getting to Paris.*

# NATURAL LIGHT
October 2001 – January 2002

The leaf is the tree he thinks, and the tree is the earth. But still they are separate. Frank is in Grant Park, with his crutch beside him. Skyscrapers lunge upward in the downtown city hub. Clouds scurry to avoid them. Frank is in a morphine haze, the medicine supplied by doctors to combat the pain.

To his left is Lake Michigan, to his right the Windy City. Around him trees and grass. It's morning. He walks for as long as he is able these days, and has taken to sitting in this park. It's near water. Homeless men drift about, and sometimes they talk to him or wave. If only the pretty girls would do the same.

The previous Tuesday on Washington Street, he'd given five dollars to a beggar woman. She could have been forty or eighty. God bless you son she'd said to him, and his eyes moistened from a draft. His ankle throbbed with pain.

He has memorised a number of intersections, battling to get to grips with the sprawling city grid. Street names are useless he finds, it's intersections that give bearings.

His body feels light and tingling. He has more drugs for when it doesn't. Morphine, codeine, whiskey. The prescriptions for the first two are legal and correct, but the dosage for the third is one he wrote himself. The sweet Kentucky cure.

A leaf blows directly in front of him, skipping. It settles, then takes off again. He follows it with his eyes, his gaze resting on his discarded shoes and socks, placed on the grass in the sunshine. He slowly moves his ankle.

He is plagued by ideas of a perfect alternative life. He gets lost in constructions and conceits. Other places, perfect people. Things hidden. Maybe it's just the injury, the morphine and being alone. Maybe it's just today. He feels that in his life he can never say goodbye, can never leave to drift what is meant to float away. His rubs his forehead with his fingertips.

A group of school children walk past. Boys and girls, laughing pushing, five or six years old. That was Frankie one time. He clicks his tongue in disgust at this mawkish sentimentality, drugs and pain or not. He puts his shoes and socks on.

Walking back across Madison Avenue and into the city, he feels a shudder at the corner of Monroe and State. His right leg buckles. He grips his crutch, his body shaking. Someone stares in alarm.

Frank stands still, recovering from the shock and relaxing his muscles. It's cooler here, with skyscrapers blocking the light. He sees a man get off a bus, his left leg severed at the knee. It makes him feel pathetic, and snaps away his self-pity.

He hobbles down the steps of the subway station, passing through the ticket barrier. The blue line will take him to Jefferson Park. There are crowds on the platform, and he's self-conscious and totally alone.

The train comes and they shuffle aboard. No vacant seats, and he hopes he won't fall and embarrass himself. Somebody would get up if he asked them, but he wants this even less.

It rattles and shakes through the tunnels, leaving the Downtown area and emerging overground. It's northwest all the way. Soon he will be home, in tree-lined squirrel suburbia. His aunt and uncle's house. A deaf man passes out key rings, as the train lets off at Belmont. Four more stops to go.

Karen got lost on the Metro. She was sure she had counted correctly, but maybe there was something she'd overlooked. Things were tricky in a new town. She had seemingly emerged at Barbes instead of Anvers, and she could hear the sound of some type of market.

A fist dug into her back. He was saying something, scouring her pockets, tiny flecks of spit flicking on her cheek. She froze, motionless. His other hand rifled her jacket, her jeans, and the fist pressed against her.

A whore, a bitch, he was calling her these names, and while she understood it, she couldn't form a reply. Her mouth refused to move. His free hand punched her hip, and in that moment she was aware of letting go of her stick. She felt her fingers open, but didn't hear it fall. Saliva prickled her neck now.

This man behind her smelt of aniseed. His arm around her waist, his fist still in her back. His right cheek touched her left. Then he was gone, or maybe he was gone for a moment, before she realised. Her body was shaking and taut.

She shook and sobbed, and felt her skin grow warmer. Not just her skin, but beneath it. Her tears were warm on her face. She cried and shook convulsively, the world receding and gone. Then the everyday life sounds were audible again - cries, shouts, buses. Somebody's dog sniffed her leg.

She moved to her left and leaned against a wall. She wiped at the tears on her face. The sounds on the street were clear as a bell, the scuffing of shoes, the coughs. Karen was totally alone. She felt in her pocket and her wallet was gone. Her money and ID.

She started walking. She returned to the metro confused but determined, and moved down the passage in what she hoped was the right direction. She asked someone near her on the platform. On the train she started relaxing. Janey had warned her about this area. Barbes, La Chapelle, Chateau Rouge.

She got off near Janey's apartment, at Ternes. She relaxed further amidst opulence. Remembering the turns to be taken, she reached rue Fourcroy, and entered the building. Janey was still at work. Karen got some water and sat down on the sofa.

She felt sensations of him touching her. Her elbows and forearms grew tight. She braced herself on the couch, and trembled some more for a while. Warmth spread. Janey returned and they spoke of the ordeal. Karen cried a little.

"I know some people who've had stuff stolen up there. Let me ring the bank and cancel the credit card, so that's one thing you don't have to worry about. It'll only take a second."

Karen let her do it. She felt so tired, and the prospect of moving at all was unwelcome. She heard Janey's voice from the bedroom. Karen had made contact with various companies online before travelling, and the response to her cv so far had been good. As soon as she signed a contract, Janey said there'd be no problem finding an apartment.

She settled back in the softness. Her body was heavy as concrete. It was good to be here, despite today's fright, and she sensed in her heart that the future was strong. Karen was in Paris two weeks.

Johnny was loathe to admit it. He wanted her. He wanted her and he couldn't have her, and it growled in his body like an unfed dog. He scowled in their general direction.

She was lounging on the piazza with her legs draped over his. Some hairgel hip boy. Her shoes had been kicked off. Johnny watched them, this random unknown couple, lounging. He hurt from craving, looking at her there, and wanting her right now. He didn't even know who she was.

She had a blue top and black dress, and was blond. Her shoes were white. The guy had some chain round his neck, a whitey down in the 'hood of his head. He was propped up on one elbow.

"Sacrifice!" roared Johnny, picking up the guitar and forming an E. "Sacrifice tonight yeah."

The autumn sun caught his watch face. He loved this Parisian autumn. In a few months it would be too cold here, and he would abandon the routine till the new year.

*"Sacrifice, for what we have's not what we need yeah,*
*Sacrifice, oh no!"*

The police idled by. They studied him carefully. One of their radios barked. Deciding against hassling him, they passed on, and he stopped playing and lit a smoke.

"Sacrifice, you fucking pigs," he muttered.

That girl was still down there. Her legs were long and tanned. He blew a smoke ring, and accepted what could not be. Still, now he had that feeling, and he'd have to find another.

His smoke ventured out into the world, drifting, fading. His phone received a text. A brown and crumpled leaf attached to his boot, and then skitted onward again.

Johnny felt like a stranger here, just for a moment, before he stopped and remembered. This was home now. This place and no other.

He checked the text and deleted it. That client was a client no more. Whenever he felt suspicious, he dropped them without hesitation. If he got in trouble here there was nowhere else to go.

**116**

He stood up and stretched his calf muscles. Kicking at the air, he saw the couple get up and move off. She was not so pretty after all. Her face held a sluttish plainness, and a dissatisfied lipcurl. Her eyes were the beads of a magpie.

Johnny spat on the ground, and worked stiffness from his limbs. He swivelled his arms and his shoulders. Blood pumped, and he felt warmer, looser. Maybe today was a good one.

He sat back down and sang for an hour, barely ending one song and beginning another. People stopped to listen before moving on. A tiny child ran up and put a coin on his knee, and as she did so she gave a sneeze. He smiled in spite of himself. "Bless you little girl," he said, and she laughed and didn't know why. Her mother beckoned her toward her.

Aria was late for the lesson. She ran down the corridor, dropping books and sheets, and her trainers made a squeaking sound. She entered the classroom and sat down.

This was the last October they would be in school. Laura had mentioned this earlier, and Aria laughed gladly, not thinking of it that way. Come next June they were finished. She found the right page in the geography book, and tried but failed to relax. She had 200 dollars in her pocket.

She had come home late the night before, shaking and drunk. She'd been nervous before the shoot. Some whiskey had calmed her, and she'd posed in the way they asked, feeling a strange adrenalin high from their stares.

Today she felt stressed-up and guilty, and wanted to do it again. It was always like this. Her mind was a swirl full of chatter, and the teacher couldn't hope to compete. Aria was lost in her thinking.

Later in the cafeteria, she ate a little. It was nice but she just didn't want it. Pushing away the plate, she got up and went to her locker. She put the money inside. There was a picture of her mother and Anna there, tacked to the back of the door, but Aria didn't want to see it now, and shielded her left eye with her hair. She slammed the door.

She skipped the next class but went to the following, and it was boring and hard to keep still. She chewed on her pen as she listened.

Math made no sense right now. Her heartbeat was getting annoying. She jiggled her knees, but that moved the desk, and soon other students were watching. She fidgeted.

"You can leave if you won't stop that fidgeting."

She stopped. This was a stupid way for a teacher to address a seventeen year old she thought, but it shamed her into stillness. She scowled at the math on the board.

"I'm doing this for you Aria," said the teacher.

At home she lay in her bedroom. She was getting more tired each day. Her lips twitched, and her limbs jumped. She struggled with imagery unwanted.

This was not a great life, she knew that. Something was definitely wrong, but maybe this work could correct it. She felt it might wash it away.

The room seemed to swim. Her head throbbed. She sat up and her fists clenched, and she inhaled deeply. Fuck these feelings she thought. If this was how it was to be, fuck it. She didn't have a clue what was wrong with her, and slumped back down in a heap. Her shoulders and neck felt so stiff.

Frank was holding the baby. His name was Jack and he was seven months old. He waved his arms and shouted with joy. His smile showed a tooth in the gum base.

"Ah sure go on outta that now," said Frank, amusing them both. "What would you be talkin' about at all at all?"

Jack bounced and tried to look at several things at once, and Frank put him down, and he sat there eyeing a soft ball. Frank got it for him. The sun was coming in and stretching on the wooden floor, the American street half visible through the blinds. A pick-up truck trundled by, going the wrong way down a one-way street. Frank laughed.

"When are you going to start walking around?" asked Frank. Jack smiled, and handed him the ball. One of the dogs arrived and sniffed at them. Frank picked Jack up and took him outside, and they admired berries in the front garden while a squirrel scampered up a tree. Jack turned his head toward the movement.

There was a church a few doors down, 'the opposition' his uncle joked. Anglican or Methodist or some form of Protestant worship. The wine just stayed wine for them there. Frank and Jack watched a woman enter, Jack's fingers catching on Frank's shirt. Frank felt a stab in his ankle.

The crutch was not needed to walk in the house. It was for downtown, or the shop. If there was no tobacco, no papers, and he was going to have to eat the grass or do without. If the dogs needed walking in the evening.

Jack wriggled and struggled, and Frank placed him on the ground. He picked at a daisy, muttering some sound to himself. Frank stepped onto the pavement. The street was straight in each direction, tree-lined, peaceful. The houses were pretty and low. It was funny to be here, to be in America in daylight, a natural clearness in the October sun. It was funny and strange.

He felt the morphine buzz, a sealing warmness, and looked up at the sky as a plane flew overhead. The house was right under the flightpath. He remembered the flat in Berlin had been too.

Jack shouted something, and Frank turned around. Jack was holding the daisy. Frank picked up a leaf and threw it at him, and Jack watched it float toward his face, making no attempt to stop it.

"That was a leaf," said Frank. Jack laughed, gurgling.

"That was a leaf that I threw at you."

Frank wandered over to a bush in the garden, and Jack watched him. A man on a bike cycled past. There was a chocolate wrapper entangled in the branches, and a fly crawled along it.

"Did you put that wrapper in the bush there?" said Frank. He walked back to where Jack was. "Did you put that wrapper in the bush?"

Jack looked at him sweetly, aware that these questions were playful.

"Did you put that wrapper in the bush there?" said Frank again, bending down and tickling Jack's ribcage. "Cause if you didn't, who did?"

He picked him up, and they went inside.

In the evening, Frank and his uncle had a beer in the basement. They sat at the old bar on barstools, studying the chessboard by lamplight. Frank was in trouble.

His queen was gone, a bishop too, and all of his enemy's pieces had cordoned off routes of attack. He moved forlornly.

"Are you sure you want to do that?" said Danny.

"I reckon I might have you if you do."

Frank placed it back.

"I think you've probably got me anyway."

"I suppose that it's lookin' that way."

They played on for a while, and Dan won. He cracked his knuckles in victory.

"I better go upstairs for a bit," he said. He finished his can and left.

Frank looked around, at the couch and the exercise clutter. A stationary bike and a treadmill. He stepped up on the treadmill and started walking at a low setting, loosening his ankle and making it warm. He liked the sensation at this pace.

There was a mirror over the far side. He watched himself, walking, and he thought he looked so thin. His forehead was creased into a frown. Consciously relaxing it, he realised how it was always like this now, furrowed, tight. He loosened his elbows and shoulders.

A dog padded on the floorboards overhead. He heard the scratch of its nails. Then the other one followed, more a scamper or a run, and Frank stretched out his arms, feeling tension ease.


In bed he lay with his discman. The comfort of low Leonard Cohen. Show me slowly what I only know the limits of, dance me to the end of love. He touched a tear on his cheek.

The room was bathed in Chicago blue. His crutch leaned against the wall. He sat up and turned off the music, and there was perfect silence. He put the headphones on the quilt. The streetlight in the laneway flickered outside, leaning over the chain link fence of the garden.

Frank watched all this stillness, like a Hopper tableau he thought, brought to life. What joy in a pure lack of motion. The streetlight died. Frank and the world did not move. He yawned, and a delivery van pulled up. Brown. UPS. The driver got out with a package, and entered a building. Then he came out and drove off again.

The night had become early morning. Frank felt pain in his leg. He leaned over for two codeine tablets, and swallowed them with water. The taste of the water was stale.

He lay back down and pulled the covers. The discman was next to his head. The headphone wire touched his neck, but he pushed it away with his eyes closed. A bird broke the silence with song.

Soon his uncle would let the dogs out. They would chase down the steps out the back. Frank was partitioned from the back door by curtain, and he heard it open every morning, and felt air. When the dogs went to piss it made him have to.

She'd moved in the day before. It was near St. Sulpice. She was still organising things, shifting the furniture around. She picked up an ashtray and placed it back down. Janey had friends who were smokers.

Karen was having a flat-warming this Friday night, in two days time. There was work to be done before that. Unpacking, arranging, some decoration. Home-making.

In the kitchen she drank some water, rubbing the sink surface. Allowing all these things become familiar. She walked around on the linoleum slowly, and there were places that squeaked and places that didn't. There was a lump near the doorway.

Janey had promised to bring plenty of people, because Karen knew nobody else. She smiled to herself, dusting a shelf, and wondered who might turn up. She tied back her hair with a band.

She thought of the man who attacked her, but didn't feel anything now. It was past and irrelevant. In the evening she hung her Beirut picture on the wall. It still held the soul of her grandfather. She went for a walk and returned feeling fresher, eager for newness and life. The fridge hummed.

So this was her new city, and the neighbourhood felt right. Central. She'd lived in the suburbs back home. She was close to the river here, and she planned on walking there often.
A fly buzzed.

She was looking forward to her job. The challenge. To the people, the new experience.
Her Mom called and asked questions. It was nice to recount what she'd done. She left out the attack altogether, because Mom would have jumped on a plane. Karen described her apartment, where all her items would go. She liked this.

When the call ended she went to bed.  It was late. Outside on the street two lovers were fighting, the woman berating the man. Karen was asleep when they reconciled.

Frank's cousin Paul went to heaven. Frank and Danny took a pew. There were great uncles, distant aunts, second cousins, and crying girls. Frank had met Paul occasionally, as a child at weddings and christenings, when Paul had flown to Dublin. He'd been kind and simple and strange.

Frank felt some pain in his ankle. He gripped the crutch. He was morphined for the morning, gazing serenely at the rituals and robes. Dan dropped his keys and they clattered on the floor.

After, groups gathered and whispered. Efforts were made to ignore the inappropriate comments of children. Frank met his relatives randomly, some known, others not, the rest half-recognised from pictures. One of them commented on his sideburns.

Driving home, they stopped off for fast food. Dan outlined the family tree. The history of the bloodline on Frank's mother's side was long in Chicago and New York. Frank listened with interest, conjuring up images of the dust bowl and before, uncaring of whether this was relevant or not. The harshness was romantic.

There were alcoholic layabouts and eyes filled with tears. Journeys across country in the snow. There were marriages that were scorned and religions renounced, and Frank thought of uncles in sharp pinstripe suits.

Back on the road the highway was clear, and Frank found a station for the religious right. They listened momentarily to the brimstone and bile, until suddenly it wasn't funny anymore. The silence was better.

"So why did you come here?" Frank asked.

"For the change."

They drove on, and Dan continued.

"I was fed up in London, with the people and my job, and when I finally got my green card, that was it. There was no hesitation." Frank rotated his ankle.

"And did you sort out a flat?"

"I stayed with my cousin, Maire. She was at the funeral too."

"For long?""Yeah, for a while. My first flat, I shared it with Rachel."

The American landscape flashed by as they went, all concrete and build-up, with wide spaces off in the distance. The highway was flanked by auto dealerships and hamburger restaurants. The El passed alongside as they came up towards home, and Frank heard the rattle, though his window was closed. The track was shaking.

In the living room they told Rachel about the funeral, and Jack sat on her knee, listening. His eyes moved from one to the other. He dropped his spoon and peered down at it curiously. It was gone and that was fine. One of the dogs shuffled over to inspect it, wondering if it was food and leaving when it wasn't. It sneezed as it left.

They drank in the basement in the cool afternoon, and Dan told a story of when Paul took him out drinking. Some dive-bar on the southside. It had been winter time, snowing, and Paul had got really drunk.

At night Frank walked the dogs. He limped around with the crutch and a can of Old Style, and they padded ahead in the moonlight. The streets were like a beautiful dream, the trees in front gardens lonely and leaning.

The evenings were still fine, but they'd soon grow much colder. Then freezing. He had hats and gloves in his wardrobe. He'd been warned before coming, pack plenty that's warm, and he'd done so obediently.

All of the houses were fronted with wooden porches. Hanging in some of these were lanterns, and some held a wicker chair. Frank moved by slowly, stopping if needed, and studied them. He was happy here in this winter world.

As he eased round the block, he came to the bridge, and stood solitary upon it. The El passed underneath. He made out a large group of young people within, students no doubt, on their way downtown for drinking. He finished his can, dropping it in a bin.

The dogs breathed beside him, and the train sound diminished till the silence returned. It was gorgeous. Frank on the bridge felt like the lord of the nightworld, the sentry of silence and of being alone.

"Come on," he whispered. "We're going back to the house." They bounded ahead into stillness. He followed in wonder, alive to it, a man with his dogs and with sweet nothing else. The morphine in his bloodstream made his heart slow and steady.

Back in the house, Frank went to the basement, and with nobody down there he rolled up a joint. He drank Ten High Kentucky bourbon before sleeping. The ice melted slowly in the glass.

He was reading a story about memory. He was melancholic from the subject and the drink. He thought of Berlin, of his life and his leaving, and put down the glass on the locker to his right.

With the room dark once more, the world disappeared. It was sealed off and separate. Frank closed his eyes and rotated his ankle, and a sharp line of pain shot right up through his knee. He felt tingling, then nothing further.

Johnny got out while she slept there. Got back on the street in a rush. Outside he wandered aimlessly, walking down rue du Ranelagh, and reaching Avenue du President Kennedy. He ambled alongside the river.

He continued down Avenue de New York, reaching Place de l'Alma. He was hot now. He couldn't decide whether to take the metro, or just keep walking. He troubled someone for a smoke. He ventured on, passing the Invalides and Alexandre III bridges, and stopped at the obelisk of Place de la Concorde.

He walked nearer and wished he hadn't, feeling ridiculous when some tourist requested a photo. But then it made him smile. Why not oblige these people, take their picture and be part of their lives. Enhance or establish a memory.

He began hoping he'd be asked again, and then he was, by a bubbly Japanese couple. He positioned them and made them say cheese. The wind took up out of nowhere, and laughs splintered lost in the gale. Half-heard, and disappearing.

Johnny sat on a wall, and watched as the people moved on. New ones arrived in the meantime. He cleared his throat and spat phlegm on the pavement, coughing. A child skipped on by like a song.

Back home he called Melissa. She came around soon after. They got into bed, but when he was about to come he pulled out, not wanting relief in her view. He went to the toilet and groaned as he jacked off into the bowl.

She made coffee and he cut his fingernails.
"Tu penses qu'on peut etre ensemble?" she said.
He ignored her and answered the phone.

Night fell and he'd done nothing. The light bulb refused to go on. He'd been here alone since the phone call, four and a half hours previously. He stretched out his hands in the dark.

On the street he felt marginally better. It was rare he just went for a walk. He passed down rue Doudeauville, with some unfortunate lying injured outside a kebab shop. He was moaning away to himself. Johnny turned left and kept going, passing the metro station, and hitting rue de Clignancourt.

He crossed over into Montmartre.

He took rue Custine, climbing steeply, and approached the Sacre Coeur from behind. The lights of it were like a beacon. There were a few people around, and he leaned on a fence looking down. The vast Parisian basin. Lights flickered everywhere, twinkling, and sparkled along the sides of the Tour Eiffel. He yawned.

There was not much to think at that moment. He thought it best to just stand there and stare. He saw the multi-coloured pipes of the Centre Pompidou, the lights of Notre Dame, the river. This was home.

In the flat he boiled some water. Drank it to warm up his bones. A spider scuttled along the sink edge, and vanished through a crack. Johnny climbed into his bed.

Karen was happy on Sunday. A smoke-smell remained on the living room furniture, but Friday night's party could be deemed a success. There was rain falling.

She'd spoken at length with a man called Michel, and agreed to give him her number. He'd told of his upbringing in Bordeaux, his hopes, his fears, and she'd been drawn in by this openness, which was not like guys back home. Neither was his evident interest in her. Perhaps because of this, or just the buzz of a gathering, she felt so light today, remembering the feel of that night and its friendly strangers.

Janey rang and gossiped about everyone, asking Karen's opinions and fishing for thoughts on Michel. Karen was diplomatic. Rain hit the window pane in swishes. Karen said goodbye and was silent.

All she heard now was the rain, a delicate brushing cadence. Then a car passing. She got up and walked about the apartment. She put on her raincoat but took it off again, not wishing to go outside. A lone bird began to screech somewhere.

She got a whiff of Michel's aftershave, from the sensory memory bank, and smiled to herself briefly, half-embarrassed to feel so girlishly young. She felt her heart beating.

Aria cried in the changing room. Her body did not feel like her own. Laura was at her French class, always talking of Paris now, but Aria needed her. She was overwhelmed and alone. Laura was going after the SAT's, and had been preparing for a long time. Already they were into November.

Aria wanted to go with her. She felt like maybe she could. She could run from all of this, her feelings and her life, and be whole again. New. In the changing room the other students chatted, and she covered her face with her hands. She smelt a gym smell.

June was when Laura was leaving. June 2002. Aria whispered it softly. She could push through the pain until that time, and then freedom. Was it possible? She hated seeing her mother and sister, hated how clearly they loved her, and she raged and shook and cried in her bedroom. Her mother cried too. "We should talk about this honey," she'd plead with her. "You can tell me whatever you're feeling."
Aria would scream.

She would clench up near-frozen and death-like, powerless as her father's hands touched her five year old body. She couldn't banish the memory. In her room with the door locked and her heart like a stone, she lay tense limbed.

Anna banged on the door, but Aria physically couldn't open it. She lay paralysed. Whenever this happened she saw many things, all flashing in her mind like a dream. Sometimes she saw a pink toy rabbit. This rabbit brought a peace when it came to her, but she mentally pushed it away. And then the hands touched her.

She was paralysed there in her bedroom, the fingertips touching her hard. Why was she seeing this now she wondered. She had been five years old, an infant, and had time not rendered it void? Was it not nothing to her now?

Frank began walking naturally. Unaided by the crutch he would walk around the block, moving at a pace that facilitated correct walking. If he went too fast he regressed to a form of hobbling, but at a slow gait the muscles seemed to work properly. His ankle clicked and protested.

The dogs sometimes accompanied him, in daylight or the evening, and all the houses were festooned and joyful, with Christmas lights, Santas, mistletoe. It was the holiday season.

In his heavy jacket and his woolly hat and gloves, Frank trudged through the snow tracks delicately. One of the dogs disappeared through a hedge, only to re-emerge covered in snow. A car skidded.

In his room Frank warmed himself, rubbing his hands and rolling his neck. He smelt chicken roasting. Rachel and Jack were in the kitchen, Jack banging on a pot, and Frank listened quietly, feeling at ease.

He took the garage route to the basement, entering by the side door, and had a smoke in the gloom. There were mice in the walls.

Their presence had been detected three days previously, when Frank noticed teeth marks in stored Irish chocolate bar wrappers, and had then seen three of them, scurrying across the floor. Dan was out buying poison. Frank looked around carefully, but knew it was unlikely he'd see them again. Their hiding places were infinite.

He stubbed out the joint, but remained seated. He took in the sense of the room. With his eyes closed and his head lolling, he sensed its parameters, sonically, spatially. He heard a dog padding above.

"You should go out and get a Yank bird," said Dan at dinner, and Rachel pretended to scold him with her eyes.

"Fly the flag for Ireland."

Frank smiled, feeling this would be a tricky proposition, but unable to deny to himself his body wanted it. Her nationality would have made no difference.

He would have lain her down and turned her around, but his mind was snapped out of it when Dan hit him with a tea towel. "Finish your chicken or I'm giving it to the dogs."

Frank washed the dishes with the cd player spinning. Nick Cave and the Bad Seeds. He saw them in Berlin, saw Tom Waits too. He pushed suds from a Celtic-patterned hotplate.

The kitchen in the evenings had become a special time. He liked washing the dishes with music playing. His mind would drift and float from him, memories, imaginings. Thoughts like slow ponderous beings.

Tonight he was thinking of Dublin, the kebabs and the piss and the puke. Smoking and drinking, slappers in skirts. It was like an English city there he thought, hardly different at all. The lager, the aggression, the frantic coupling with strangers in the streets. He'd done that too, like anyone.

He finished the dishes and went to his room, then to the basement to smoke. The bag of grass was getting lighter, nearly 300 dollars of it in his lungs. It was sweet though. It was sweet and made him melancholic, and slowed his mind. He stretched his arms upward.

He got a can of Old Style from the fridge, and cracked it open with a groan. Then he guzzled from it.

Jack stood up by the fireplace. Terminator 2 was on television, as he rose shakily near the grate. Frank watched him curiously, feeling sure this was the very first time – an unassisted standing being accomplished. Jack waved his arms, shouted, and then folded neatly onto his bottom. "Silence," ordered Schwarzenegger on screen.

Rachel and Dan were out, and Frank the babysitter was drinking a beer. He smiled at Jack. There was a crash on the screen and Jack's head swivelled, his eyes wide as saucers. "That was a crash," said Frank. Jack watched him and listened. He crawled over towards Frank and gripped the edges of the couch. Frank picked him up and they sat together, Jack chewing a toy.

"I'm going to be leaving soon," said Frank. I'm going to be going away."

Jack went asleep in his arms later, and Frank watched his innocent face, his sighs and his nasal breath-flow. His mind didn't know of sadness. What would his life hold, what would Frank's, and if they ever met again, would the sleeping child remember?
Was he dreaming?

Frank turned off the tv. The walls were painted yellow, a warm and vivid hue, and he took in the room slowly, deliberately. Jack shifted for an instant. There was pain in Frank's body, and the doctors had said there would be forever. There was breakage and deformation. He looked at this sleeping boy on his chest, and smiled at his energy. His boundless, shouting glee.

When Dan and Rachel came home the dogs would start barking. Jack would probably wake for a moment, and then sleep again. Would wake without knowing he had done so. One of the dogs ventured over, silent and wagging its tail, and Frank patted the soft dark head, two loving eyes regarding him.

He closed his eyes and relaxed. He was almost holding himself. It was like he had his arms around his own sleeping form, protecting it from everything, everywhere. He felt his pulse throbbing.

The arrival of Dan and Rachel was imminent. Frank sat on the couch with the baby in his arms, the dogs alongside him, and his history like a trail. He had a life to live through.

Karen met Michel at her metro station. He had bags of Christmas presents bundled in his arms, and she offered to carry one but he refused. He asked her to accompany him northward.

On the train they spoke about Christmastime, and Michel said it was his favourite time of year. The carriage rumbled and shook. He wanted to go to Chateau Rouge, saying he had a present for a friend there. After, they could walk in Montmartre.

When they got to the station they pushed up the stairway, Michel guiding her with his voice. One of his parcels touched against her for a second, and he apologised, sounding out of breath. They emerged into bustle, and walked noisy, crowded streets at a slow pace. She knew this was near her attack site. Michel apologised again, saying it wouldn't be much longer, and then they were stopped on the pavement, and he was shouting up at somebody.

A gruff voice answered, and came down to open the door. Karen heard a rustling interplay, the giving of the gift presumably, and then Michel was introducing her, saying this was Johnny. Johnny asked her nationality, and spoke English out of courtesy. She didn't bother mentioning she spoke French. Michel did, saying he couldn't understand, but Johnny ignored his pleas for a language switch, and talked so much Karen couldn't hope to initiate one. They chatted about the weather.

She felt comfortable in his presence, temporarily forgetting Michel, and concentrating on the voice. It was rough hewn, scraped, story-filled. He said he was Senegalese, a musician, and the harsh Northern weather had sandpapered his skin. She asked where he learned his English.
"It's like gravel my skin, can you feel it?"
Before she knew it her hand was raised, touching his face, unknowing as to whether it had reached or been placed there. She rubbed his cheek.

Michel coughed awkwardly.
"Tu veux partir, cherie? Il est tard."
They left. They travelled back to St. Sulpice, neither saying very much, and she wondered in her head what fire she was feeling. It was otherworldly.

Michel gave her some presents to carry this time, and they ventured up the stairs into the night.

Later, alone, her mind returned to Johnny's face. The feel of his skin. In his voice lay authority, mystery, desperation. She had wondered then how his eyes were, and had never really dwelled on this in meeting someone before. She had learnt it didn't matter.

She turned over and tried to sleep, and did so after a spell. But the lurching of her dreamscape awoke her. She sat up in her nightdress, the covers half falling, permitting stabs of cold. Her muscles ached. Half awake, she thought three things, and got up to find her computer so she could write them down.

Life was the thrust of the everyday.

Death was the shrinking from life.

Rest and good food lead to peace.

*If you invite pain and suffering into your life, they will come running. Don't invite them he thinks, just deal with them if they come.*

*Djinn had seen his mother raped. In the kitchen, near a chair. He'd been young, a child only, watching wide-eyed and unmoving. When their business was finished the rapists left. He'd run to her, held her, cried as she cried with him, on the tile floor. This was long ago.*

*He stands by the window on this French suburban street. He is in the town of Malakoff, next to Paris. A car goes by at a slow speed, two smiling children in the backseat. Djinn rubs at his eyelids.*

*Over in Beirut he had the sounds that helped to mould him. The familiar floating noise. Here he feels unmoved by it, the music of daily life, taking nothing from the French cars, voices, bird calls. He wishes he could block them out.*

*He has been living here a month. It is the second of October 2003, and he feels like he's been here forever. The days are long and tedious. He has tramped the streets and consulted maps, pinpointed useful locations. Has surveyed the site many times. He has looked from every possible angle, calculated distances, ascended often as a tourist. The Tower of Montparnasse. He knows it like a body part.*

*On their buses he stares out the window. On their trains he looks straight ahead. He ignores their old people, their words, their sinful immoral girls. He prays. On the streets his tension hurts him, muscular folds tightening in his shoulders and back. He stretches his joints in the evenings.*

*Once a woman asked him the time. He acted like he hadn't heard her. If he caught someone's eye he would glance at the floor, or away, anywhere. It made his head sore. The weather was harsh, filling his soul with anger and fear. Making his skin crack.*

*He reads from his Qur'an and recites his prayers turned
eastward. He eats silently. To control a plan he knows one must
control oneself, and this can only be done by adhering to routine.
If a bird sings he denies the occurrence, struggling to banish the
memory of a simple, once pleasant event. The tea they sell here
distresses him.*

*The clock is ticking on and the time is fast approaching.
Patience will offer reward. He senses something massive, far
beyond his scope. French cars, French people, French steel and
glass and skin. All will crumble, melt, burn in holy flame, like a
prophecy. He feels tired.*

*He lies on his bed and stares at the ceiling. There is a crack
with an insect upon it. The creature follows the line of the fissure,
almost exactly, creeping upside down. Djinn follows it with his
eyes.*

*He will sleep later, dreaming of death. To dream of death is
important. It means his heart is pure, his mind focused, his soul
is free from fear. It means his will will carry him. He must die too
he believes, in the building he will hit. His soul must mingle with
the others. He turns off the lamp in his bedroom.*

# THINGS AS THEY ARE

Don't let the swirl of desire be your master. Johnny knew this, but it was easy to forget. His longed for October light was upon him again, the years slipping by, his hopes and fears still with him. He watched the students up in the Pompidou library, their busy forms moving back and forth, and he down below on the tile stones. Johnny with pigeons and chill.

He waved his arm and he was just with the chill, and some moments later with Michel. Within an hour he was alone again. He stood up and rubbed his stiff legs, and picked up the guitar, figuring that was enough for today. He went to a café for a beer.

The waitress was familiar to him from a cold night, and he'd known this would be so before entering. He sat with his back to her. She approached and was shocked momentarily, but then recovered, and merely took his order in sadness. Her eyes were like pools built from loss.

Johnny drank with a listlessness, breathing heavier than he needed to. He knew he was holding her interest. He felt her attention on his back and the back of his head, a laser beam of embarrassment, and disappointment, and ruin. Another waitress with tear stains.

He left as the dark became resolute, walking down Boulevard de Sebastopol with the beer buzzing. Early evenings cloaked in blackness. He stopped into a sex shop, and bought a magazine full of girls with their legs spread. Young blondes probably distant from their fathers. On the street with it in his jacket pocket, he waited patiently at the lights till the colour changed, and crossed to go east on rue Reaumur. He sat down at Republique.

People hurried cloaked in distractions, thinking of their lover or their kettle or their bills. Johnny stretched out like a cat. He watched some kids on a makeshift merry-go-round, two Arabs controlling the motor and selling candyfloss as a sideline. Mothers watched their children on horses.

There was one time in Paris when he got called a nigger, by an American bouncer outside a club. Soon after his arrival. It had not hurt or surprised him, but the sensation of powerlessness was strong. He could only walk away down the queue length.

He was reminded of this for no reason, or no reason he was able to detect. He was reminded, and forgot, and it was lost again.

Things are as they are he knew, and he couldn't sit forever. He stood up and shook himself, meandering slowly back toward Chateau Rouge. Was this city a burden to him now? It was too familiar, too known to him, too mocking of his weakness and his exiled raging heart. He knew the dogshit stains.

He was on rue de Chabrol, and then rue la Fayette, crossing over onto rue du Faubourg Poissoniere. He bought another beer in a fruit shop.

Nothing could lift his despondency tonight. These streets were boring now, and useless. They were the hunter's net of all his failures and insecurities, the recording apparatus of his conquest born from need. They were unmerciful. He heard an argument from a window up above him, woman wailing husband drunk. He spat saliva mixed with Kronenbourg.

Rain would have spoken for his misery. There was none. Crashing, smashing fucked off rain would have given voice to his anger, have bellowed where he was mute, but nothing but a breeze lived, and it was cool and gentle.

Aria saw the graveyard boy on the subway. He saw her too, but she didn't know that. She found herself looking repeatedly, which was strange, because since that day she hadn't thought of him at all. He looked fuller, more whole now.

She gently made him notice her, watching until he had to glance up. She wanted to show she remembered him. He remembered her too, trying and failing to conceal this in his eyes, and she studied them, and knew.

They got off the train in slow motion, her from one door him another, and sat down on metro benches, silently. They were twenty metres apart. The station emptied like sink-water, passengers gurgling and spilling through the gates, and finally Aria's trainers made echoing squeaks as she jigged. Frank watched her minute nervous movements.

"Tu parles francais ou anglais?"

"Les deux."

"But English is how you were born."

"Yeah," she laughed, finding the sentence amusing.

He stood up and shuffled much closer.

When he was standing before her she smiled at him, and he smiled back without fear.

Some people appeared on the platform, scattered randomly along, and Frank and Aria stood up and passed though the exit. She was aware of her hair and her jawbone. Their arms touched as they moved into daylight, accidentally, or not. Both felt so strange and so calm.

The station they'd emerged at was St. Sulpice, and they sat on a bench on the church square, while pigeons inspected them for sandwiches. A man tuned a violin in the sunshine.

Frank and Aria listened to him – the half-escaping notes, which he would soon turn effortlessly to music. The instrument whinnied and conformed for him. He commenced a lilting waltz made from sorrow and rain, an inappropriate sound when two lovers have met.

It bound their first encounter with finality, reminding of transience, and endings. It didn't bother them in that moment.

Later in a cinema, with Aria drinking Coke and Frank ablaze with new care for her, they let their knees touch one another, through jean fabric. The actors emoted on screen. They sat by the river after, lost in the eyes lost in their eyes, while tourist cruisers passed. All was maintained by the light falling.
"So you think you're going to stay forever?"
"Yeah," he said. "I can't see any reason to leave."
The purple sky wrapped the day up in night-time, leaving the American girl and the Irish boy to stand wordlessly, and depart the quai-side. A dog barked from under a bridge. Frank took Aria's number carefully, writing it precisely, and clarifying twice. She smiled and her lips held him spellbound. As he walked home southward and her northeast, the dog by the river found a sandwich in a drain. He wolfed it hungrily, stale lettuce splatting on the cobbles. He sneezed from pepper mixed with dried mayonnaise, rubbing at his snout with his right front paw.

Karen was sure he took something. The summer feeling had not gone away, and by August she'd decided that her boyfriend was on drugs. This certainty played havoc with her sleeping.

She was at work with her mind elsewhere, tossing and returning to her thoughts. She spoke on the phone to her clients. She flicked through the same thoughts, repeatedly.

Could she help him if she left him?

Would he hate her if she tried?

Did she know what she was talking about, and know what she was feeling, and was it really dreadful if her boyfriend took some drugs?

These were crashing questions often.

She walked by the river keeping distant from the bank, along the cobbles. She could hear the Right Bank traffic. The water made aching lap sounds, salivating against the rock slope below her. She smelt the smoke from a cigarette.

Passing under a bridge with the echo of her steps, her foot struck something solid, and she stumbled for an instant. Recovering, leaning heavily on her stick, she was hit with a blast of pungent urine odour, the harshness overpowering in her throat and in her nose. She staggered shakily through the tunnel.

Out the other side, sweet air on her face again, she moved to her left to lean against the wall. She felt with her stick for a concrete bench she knew must be around somewhere, and finding it, sat down. Her strength returned quickly.

"Il fait beau aujourd'hui," offered someone.

"Oui," she echoed back. "Il fait beau."

She heard his footsteps receding, as he ventured on with what sounded like a small dog. The water licked and sluiced. She returned the way she had come, ascending from the quai to the roadside, and crossing at the nearby lights.

She walked down what she knew to be rue des Saints Peres, took a left onto Saint Germain and a right onto rue de Rennes, and was nearly home. Two more turns until her building.

She boiled water for tea in her apartment, and realised with a start she hadn't thought of Michel the entire time. She wished this forgetfulness would return. Trying to forget would initiate the old dance of wanting something and failing because she wanted it, so she concentrated instead on the tea-taste in her mouth. If Michel had returned than so be it.

The tea was delicately scented, a fruit and herb aroma that could clear her mind at once. She sat back and drank it slowly. Michel and her Michel options swam within her, fading, repeating, making more and less sense. She tried imagining exactly what that Beirut picture looked like.

Her cell phone rang but she ignored it, knowing today it wouldn't be Mom, and not in the mood to talk to anyone else. She heard the buzz of a text received, someone having left a message. She finished her tea, swallowing the last of it, just the taste and the smell quite faint but still there. She placed the cup on the side table.

Laura dusted the apartment. It was a cold but sunny morning, and she lifted and replaced glasses and cds, getting at the nooks and crannies with her duster and cloth.

She was happy but apprehensive for Aria with this new boy from Ireland. Aria spoke like she'd known him forever. Laura had yet to meet him. She paused for a second letting dust float around, and then resumed cleaning while a bird broke into song. There was a radio from somebody's window.

Two weeks before, Aria had come home so happy, full of joy from this Frank guy. They'd met and then gone to the movies. Laura was suspicious of anyone who spoke to Aria, though she was careful not to show this, wondering whether they sensed the same sweet vulnerability she did. In bars, did she protect or stifle Aria? She wasn't sure, but felt her intentions were good.

She dropped the cloth and knelt to pick it up, spying one of Aria's socks half-trapped beneath a chair leg. God she felt like her mother. She fished it out and threw it in the wash pile, and laughed at herself, 20 going on 40. She suddenly felt dowdy in her flip-flops.

She felt Aria's French was so good now. Laura watched out for her when they went out, but thought sometimes she needn't. The knowledge of what Aria had been through made her do so. She had been hurt, and she was younger.

Laura saw herself as the girl who made you laugh to show she loved you, but the boys she'd met thus far viewed such girls platonically. Lukas was an exception. Her self-appointed shepherding of Aria didn't help either. She knew she was popular with boys, could punch and mock them easily, but sometimes there were moments when that didn't seem enough. She'd found it hard to get closer.

That night she worked on a college assignment. The paper was due the next Monday. She yawned and stretched and started writing again, a girl in a window with a lamp and a desk. She heard trash cans being opened in the courtyard.

The words came easily, and she felt it would be ready for Monday. She took a break and walked slowly round the apartment, eyeing the areas she had earlier cleaned. It looked bigger with the dust gone.

She had liked Lukas, but he turned out a fool. She'd been tricked by his eyes blue and beautiful. The exotic newness of his speech and his style, the detached intelligence of his Swedishness, had led her to believe she'd found a soul of depth.

She sat back at the desk and drew a space monster, a small boggle-eyed creature in the corner of her notes. She gave him fur and a nose and whiskers. He smiled up at her, and she coloured in his fur with a purple felt-tip pen. His eyes got light blue irises. Settling back to her schoolwork, she would glance at him occasionally. Then laugh and resume writing.

When Aria came home they could drink wine together. The bottle sat on the shelf with the cork half jammed back in. Laura opened the window feeling air upon her face, and then the sound of Aria's key in the lock made her smile with joy and loosening. Her baby was back from her travels.

Michel took a hit to get started, leaving the flat more immune to the day. He felt he could easily get the bus to Chatelet and buy credit for his phone. He clenched his fists and sensed that confidence arriving.

On the bus, he watched his right leg jumping and couldn't make it stop. He heard a baby babble behind him. The other passengers included an old man and two old women, and they looked to him so happy, touching each other's arms as they spoke. He watched with his natural discretion, and wondered in awe whether they were always like this, or had something incredible happened to them today.

At Chatelet he got off, and the air-hiss let the door close. The engine revved and was distant. He stood on the street and then entered a tabac, emerging afterward with phone credit. He could do with another quick snort.

He was very near the Pompidou, and he debated dropping by Johnny or leaving it till later. He thought maybe he'd leave it until later. He walked north up rue Saint-Denis, and pushed through sexshop curtains, the gaudy facade and porn-strewn windows rendering him helpless. He went straight to the toilet, snorted, and then began browsing.

Other men shuffled around him, maybe ten in the shop, and it stretched back a little. It was easy to pretend they weren't there. He hadn't looked at any faces, hadn't noticed any items of clothing, and he was comfortable in the knowledge that they were likewise aloof. He took a quick peek at the sex-toys.

Later when he did go to Johnny, he approached him from behind, and startled him by sitting. He drew up alongside, coughed, and flopped down. Johnny had broken a string on the guitar, the B string he was saying, and Michel watched as he unhooked it, throwing the two parts away. They were all coiled up and frayed.

Johnny strode off to replace the missing string. Michel was fatigué on the piazza.

He scanned lazily about, the scenery essentially a constant, some other tourists replacing the last day's group. He thought for a time about Karen.

Johnny returned and popped a champagne bottle, a far from quality smell escaping when he did. They drank and the cold liquid made them shiver. Johnny shifted and some condoms fell out of his pocket, and he hissed in annoyance as he quickly placed them back. Michel was going to laugh but didn't.

"I recall in the summer and we did the English."

"Of course you recall," spat Johnny. "It was only a few fucking months ago."

He had bought a whole new set of strings, and he was busy ripping out the old ones. Michel watched him discard them.

"Yes, in the summer and we did the English."

Johnny raised his eyes up to heaven.

Michel stood and yawned theatrically, and Johnny turned the pegs to stretch the new strings. They'd wander out of tune for about two days now. He listened to the ascending pitch, wrestling the pegs around, so caked were they in rust. The instrument rattled and moaned.

*"I'm like a bird,"* sang Michel. *"I don't know where my home is, I don't know where my phone is."*

Johnny stared at him, horrified. Michel continued singing and Johnny tightened the strings. Together the sound was unbearable. People were gaping with pained expressions, and a beggar who was passing stuck his finger in his ear. Pigeons took off in a hurry.

*Oh yeah, yeah, yeah,* screeched Johnny. *Like a motherfucking bird.*

He twisted the pegs and clawed at the strings like a lunatic, a cacophonous racket blundering into being. Michel kept singing as he had been.

They now had the attention of probably everyone on the piazza, no one particularly welcoming of this din they were inflicting. A dog began howling like a wolf.

They kept at it for about five minutes, and when they stopped, the silence was total and eerie. It was life with an absence of volume. Gradually, people started moving and speaking again, looking in their pockets or playing with their phones. For that five minute period, Michel and Johnny had controlled the square. They smiled and returned to their drinking.

Frank watched the wall assembled. The keeper screamed inaudibly, moving the four men left, and then halting them. Guti, Beckham, Raul, and Figo placed their hands over their groins, and braced. Ronaldinho hovered, bug-eyed. Giovanni Van Bronkhurst whispered something in his ear.

The free kick came in and Casillas parried it, Salgado thumping it forward, defenders clearing their lines. Salgado seemed to be hobbling. Frank took a sip from his glass, Belgian wheat beer Leffe, and leaned a little back on his stool. The bar was deserted.

The ball went out over the Barcelona goal-line, skidding off the head of Puyol. Helguera trundled forward using elbows to gain space. Raul and Ronaldo darted and shimmied, as Luis Figo stepped up to take the corner, with two centuries of Portuguese melancholy etched into his face.

Frank ordered another. The set piece came to nothing, the game unsurprisingly tight. El Clasico. Real Madrid vs. Barcelona. Zidane did some tricks at the by-line.

So it was two weeks knowing Aria, weeks where the ground wasn't there, and he ate from the free bowl of peanuts, dreamily. Her smile made him want to do right.

He got up to drain some beer, and returned to the spectacle of Raul Bravo doing the splits. Xavi had gone down from this unorthodox challenge, and Raul Bravo didn't seem to be able to get up without assistance. Saviola scuttled about.

Frank wanted Aria to experience this with him. They could share each other's interests, joyfully. They had already spoken at length of their lives and their frailties, but he felt they each had something extra, which they hadn't mentioned yet.

He sensed into his body and felt some tension in his shoulders. He rolled them slowly around. Tendons stretched and muscles were loosened, and something gently cracked. His hair was warm on his forehead. He watched Raul give out pointlessly to Figo, as it was he himself who was playing badly. Figo batted him away.

Frank sent her a text at half time, and then sat staring at his phone for the reply to come. Seven minutes later he was satisfied. She was at home hanging out with Laura, tired after work. He imagined them there in the kitchen.

He'd first seen her apartment a week before, and she had yet to see his. Next week. He would ask her down and try to cook something, and he could meet her off the bus and drop her back. He hadn't met Laura yet, and often for him meeting someone's friends was the hardest. The girl's close companions, who s crutinise.

Madrid emerged from the interval galvanised. The game was taken to Barca in the glorious Camp Nou. Figo sprinted down the right to boos and jeers and whistles, and fired a cross to Ronaldo, who thundered it off the post. Beckham did his best to look pretty. Guti and Xavi battled for midfield supremacy, using whatever questionable methods might gain the upper hand. Ronaldinho bounced like a schoolboy.

Frank felt some pain in his ankle. He could never play this game again, even for fun in a courtyard, and although he hadn't been good the loss registered. It was restriction, lessening. He finished his beer and let the game finish too, and left. It was dark with some frost on the street.

Some guy shouldered past and demanded cigarettes, but Frank ignored him, oblivious. It was sweet to know Aria's name.

In their apartment, Aria and Laura prepared the evening meal to music. Aria chopped onion while Laura buttered bread, and the pasta bubbled slowly. They had plates and glasses set out, and wine waiting patiently on the counter.

They ate and spoke of eating, dishes they should some day attempt. Laura dipped bread in the sauce. There was steam in the kitchen from the boiling pasta water, and Laura got up mid-sentence to let in air. The chill made her soon change her mind.

Aria glanced at her, and knew immediately she wanted to steer the conversation. Towards Frank, towards nosiness. Her smile was challenging, playful.

"I don't know what you're smiling at, cause I'm not saying a word."

Laura pursed her lips.

"I'm not," repeated Aria, laughing without meaning to.

Someone slammed the lid of a bin.

Frank texted after an hour, and Laura watched, as Aria thought of her reply. He was alone in a bar watching soccer.

They talked about him then as the bottle emptied. All about the mystery of his look. Whatever she felt, it was new for this guy. He had a quality unencountered, a stance. He'd be alien in San Jose.

The night ended and they were tired. They brushed their teeth side by side at the sink. Climbing up the ladder, Aria shuddered with joy, this guy who breathed also, sending lines to her.

Karen told Michel they had a problem. He was crying when she hung up the phone. She had got right into it, her suspicions and her fears, and she knew by his reactions that she'd caught him unawares.

She cried a little herself, re-casting her mind over the conversation. She thought maybe she'd been harsh, tetchy. Still, it was killing her. Drugs was a subject foreign to her, but the change in his energy and mood was devastating. Once she'd noticed it, it was everywhere.

He had protested meekly like an infant, had pleaded with her, but she could tell. What kind of drug was it anyway? She knew of cocaine, speed – was it one of these he took? She hadn't asked, hadn't wanted to right then, but now she did, now she wondered. He put this stuff in his body.

She got up and went to the kitchen. What was her next move from here? He would call of course, but how to handle it. She didn't know who might advise her.

She drank some water and thought furiously. Her mind was racing. The water enveloped her tongue, its coldness bringing clarity, and she took deep breaths until her brain had quietened. She heard a man laughing.

I'll let things relax, she thought. The man laughed again from wherever.

Sitting on the couch she felt stressed again, so she got up and rolled her neck. Then she kneaded her fingers. These little exercises never failed, putting her back in touch with herself, her priorities. She knew worry was counter productive.

She felt the air in her nostrils, the softness of it, and she moved her hands. Her wrists bent. Her left elbow cracked as she extended her arm, feeling power and calm. Her neck grew warm and she sensed it. The hairs on her head came alive, the muscles in her calves went tight. Then her hip shuddered.

She went loose, weightless, and the pain passed. Slowly she commenced again. Her knees and thighs braced, bearing weight while she pivoted. Her spine was gently aligned.

As anxious energy vanished, she surrendered completely to the movements. Her mind didn't think or create.

It was empty, hollow, a space alive with peace. The tempo of the world was slower. She stretched and swayed hypnotically, or that's the way it seemed to her, no separation of her consciousness. She joined with the nothing outside.

Michel would call when he was ready to. Then she would know what to do.

Djinn was in the supermarket. He held a basket with fruit inside it, and read from a tin. Did he want to eat this or not? He decided to take it, placed it carefully next to the apples, and continued. An old woman stepped to one side.

In the second aisle he studied the sauces, tomato and curry and others in jars. He scanned the top shelf for rice. He wanted cereal as well as this, and walked quickly around to locate it. He avoided the brands made from sugar.

When all was bought and he was back on the street, one of his bags burst. Apples rolled drainward bound. He hated himself for his stupidity, feeling undignified scrambling about, and looked up frantically, making sure no one had seen. A little girl smiled from a window. He clenched tight his jaw, furious.

In the apartment he checked the bruising, the apples discoloured and cracked. He binned them in another wave of fury. This country, its weather and people. He ran the tap to wash apple juice from his fingertips, kneading the joints together to remove the sticky mess. The soap he was using was useless.

He left after lunch again, stalking the streets of the 14th *arrondissement*. The air was chilly and sharp. On rue Didot he felt a pain in his side, and leaned against a lamppost, gasping. A dog moved out of the way.

He ventured down roads and alleyways, weaving toward the tower he planned to hit. That day was so close he could feel it. At last he stood underneath, staring up at the lights. There were people in there oblivious. He watched the traffic on the place alongside, the stopping and starting, and the people in throngs. It was like his own movie. They came towards him, didn't see him, were replaced by others in an endless urban dance. He felt they were all the same.

He smoked a cigarette and ignored a scavenging beggar. He spat on the ground to dismiss him. Smoke curled around, escaping from Djinn's mouth. A woman eyed him malevolently.

There were dark clouds overhead now. It looked certain it would rain. Others sensed this also, scurried to shelter in time, but he didn't. He waited and then it began. Massive drops descended, splashing the concrete world.

He stood there impassive and unflinching.

"Monsieur," someone called out. "Monsieur." He ignored this completely. Soon all sound was drowned out by the rain, the passing cars and rumbling chatter unheard. He could feel his sensations shutting down. He clenched his fists and gripped his teeth with his tongue, urging feeling to return so he might suffer longer. His elbows shook.

Whenever this rain stopped he would stand for another hour. He decided it there and then. Whenever the water ceased and the world again resumed, he would stand one hour more in this place. Society or conscience wouldn't move him.

He rubbed at his face as the water thundered down, feeling stinging on his cheeks and nothing in his hands. "Monsieur!" he heard again, as from a distance.

Laura left the flat to go to college. She crossed over Republique and was soon at the Pompidou. She took Pont d'Arcole onto Ile de le Cite, and stopped for a moment beside Notre Dame, craning her neck until it hurt. The sparrows up above looked unnatural.

The Sorbonne stood between Saint Jacques and Saint Michel. She entered through the main gates. Passing through corridors and hallways, with students everywhere, she felt a buzzing in her head.

The classes were uneventful, taking her up to four o'clock, and then depositing her back on the street. She looked at cds in Gibert Joseph. There were bands she had never heard of.

One of these, The Death Monsters, had a picture of a girl being tortured. A guy pushed alongside to study it. Was he a rocker or a Goth, a nu-metaller or a punk? She found herself laughing at these labels.

She moved over to the F section, bands called Fugazi and Fish. She knew Fugazi were D.C. punks. She picked up the record, read the song titles, and saw she knew most of them to sing.

She met Lukas by the river. She was homeward bound again. "It's a difficult game for the first time writer," he said. "You have to write the book with all your heart, and then sell it like a used car." She hadn't seen him in months.

They spoke briefly as the wind blew. She wished him luck with his work, although he'd never let her read a line. She left, sensing he didn't want her too.

She didn't look back, but was aware he was still standing there. She tied back her hair as she went. She crossed Place de l'Hotel de Ville. Pigeons scattered in front of her, cooing and flapping their wings. She went up rue du Temple as the light fell, crossing and then recrossing the street. Pavements were being dug up and drilled at. This street was so familiar, this Paris life permanent now. It was strange to think she might one day leave.

There was a Chinese man dragging a mattress, scuffing it up and down kerbs. His face didn't register exertion. She wondered should she help him, and made a first step towards doing so, but the aloofness of his calm put her off.

She walked on and was soon home. She turned on the light by the door. The neighbours were preparing something spicy and exotic. She hung up her coat and sat down by the cooker, observing its rust and small cracks. She was starving to make something great.

It was the 15th of November. Soon another year would end, 2004 would usher in, and he knew he would still be here, dissatisfied. The exile alone on the square.

He spat on the ground and nearby pigeons flapped their wings. He swiped his arm angrily to disperse them, a movement which he felt defined his life. Another week and he'd leave Beaubourg till the springtime.

Johnny was not conscious of how much he missed his homeland. Sometimes, at two or three in the morning, he became so. But that was different. That was half-awake, murmuring, maybe in someone else's bed. It was unreal and forgotten by daybreak.

The night before he had dreamt of Michel's girlfriend. Of following her down the street and watching her undress. Was this unwholesome owing to her blindness? He was more concerned by this than the fact she was with Michel, and he thought it funny he should think of her when he'd only met her twice. Not for a year or more either.

He stood up and the years echoed. The history of his endless routine. He stretched, yawned, scratched at the back of his neck. He felt he would grow old performing these functions.

The wind started blowing, carrying flecks of rain. He ran to shelter under the bowels of the building, huddling near two security guards who sentried the Pompidou elevator. One of them nodded hello. Johnny took out some cigarettes and made a half-hearted gesture to offer them. Both men declined. He lit up, shielding out the wind, and dragged passionately. There was little else to do.

A Dior bag blew across the emptying piazza. A well heeled woman clattered after it. Her shoes clopped like a horse's hooves, her skirt riding up her leg. Johnny watched ambivalently, aware the guards did also.

She recovered the bag with her hair all aflutter. Johnny dropped the cigarette and spat. The guards started talking about her legs.

He left the square and went to the cinema. He paid in an abundance of change. Five and ten cent pieces, lining the pockets of his jacket. The ticket girl rolled her eyes. It was a film by Michael Mann. Heat starring Robert de Niro and Al Pacino, all alive with the mystery and beauty of the world. A heavyweight meditation, masquerading as criminals and cops. He thought it profound, breath-taking, cool and neon blue, a soundtrack like a soul humming.

Johnny watched in solitude, aching from the images. Loneliness and the drive to be lonely. He rubbed his eyes and pretended he was nowhere, a floating being unburdened, left in aesthetic contemplation.

After, he departed gingerly. He drifted down the streets feeling different and much younger, a part of him quite certain that the future wasn't dead. It just needed gentle coaxing.

Frank and Aria had dinner in Frank's place. Cleaning took him hours but he was sure it was worth it. He met her off the bus, and she looked so beautiful dismounting. He kissed both her cheeks and they embraced.

When they entered the apartment, he felt for a second like he was on some reality dating show, but then the sensation passed. Momentary nerves and anxiety. In that flash, he was positioned somewhere else, observing them, but within a heartbeat they were seated, and he melted back into himself. He was present again and content with it.

She was wearing a red cardigan that he really liked. He was going to say it but didn't. She complimented his culinary efforts, and he brushed it off and feigned indifference. Didn't tell he'd slaved that afternoon for hours. The Chilean wine was good and relaxed him further.

She asked about his leg, saying she'd noticed him limping. He told her the story without hesitation. Berlin, the bus crash, recovery both body and mind, and already he knew she related, and then she told her story too.

He poured more wine, and they paused to let things settle. There was no rush, and no need for it. Frank went to take her hand, but then decided not to. They were already joined as it was.

Outside the moon was a day from being in fullness. The same could be said for the lovers in its light. They slept together that night, first time, right time, and Frank was lost in pleasure like no other he had known. The bed creaked and made them laugh.

In the morning Aria went for *croissants*. He showered and after they ate. She'd had some funny conversation with the woman in the bakery, an impromptu discussion on men, and she was still laughing at the woman's advice, which was avoidance for life.

They turned on the radio and the sun filled the kitchen – crystal, piercing wintersun. An ad came on for the mayor's office, some concert or spectacle planned.

Frank smiled at Aria, how guileless her laughter could be, and he knew he was totally in love with her, her presence, her soul and her past.

Djinn stood by his window in the morning. Sun shone through. Across the street a girl passed slowly, and returned soon after with a bakery bag. She retraced the way she'd come, looking about at the neighbourhood. Her pastries or whatever swung at her side.

He stretched and stood a little longer. He smoked his last cigarette. Scratching at his beard he felt a sting, and realised he'd opened a cut. A circle of blood ringed his fingertip.

He left it there, feeling it dry, and walked about the room to be prepared. He'd found a job stocking shelves in a supermarket, his unwillingness to talk not a hindrance. He performed his tasks robotically, apart.

He cleaned his apartment, and washed the cloth he'd used. He hung it off the window sill. He took a bus to go to work. An Arab was staring at a white woman who climbed aboard, flicking his tongue, his eyes cold and hard. Djinn was disgusted by them both. The man for betraying himself, the other an impure bitch. He cast his eyes down in indignation.

At his stop he alighted, and strode past the security guard without greeting him. He changed in the storeroom into his red jacket and white shirt, and made his way to the soft drinks section. Stocks were running low, and he walked quickly to the stores to replenish them. A child banged into him and apologised.

Stacking the bottles in silence, he accidentally dropped one, and it bounced off the floor. He picked it up and offered it to the child, still standing alongside. He scowled and ran away.

The night he spent alone like every other. He smoked, planned, occasionally played solitaire. With a three card turnover to make it last. He reshuffled the deck and dealt again.

The ice on the ground was unpredictable. As he slipped and nearly fell, Michel cursed and grabbed a railing. He was in Jardin du Luxembourg, having just been turned down for a part in a play. He thought it wouldn't have suited him anyway.

He'd arrived for the audition early, taken a quick snort and rehearsed, but he knew the lines were no good for him, the character impenetrable and cold. Nevertheless, he'd attempted it.

It was six months since he'd found any theatre work, and he wondered sometimes was he foolish not to audition for television ads. Was it still selling out if he had no choice? Borrowing money from his parents was getting harder with each visit, his mother clucking and fretful, his father dismayed by his son. It might nearly be easier if he was angry with him.

Michel sat down, rubbing his hands and shivering. The expelled performance adrenalin had him horny. He could never think of Karen in this humour. Instead he would settle for a magazine, or recall some skinflick once viewed.

There weren't many people in the gardens. He felt savagely depressed in that moment, cold and alone on a bench, while the world carried on unaware of him. He gripped at his hands and his elbows.

Only his bones made him move again. They were aching and stiff, and so he stood up and walked to relieve them. He left by the south exit, and crossed over Saint Michel. The cold was stinging his cheeks. He jumped on a bus that was heading back north, grateful to just sit and be carried. Some teenagers slouched on and didn't pay.

The bus wound its way toward Bastille. It got caught in traffic near the quai. Michel bit his fingernails and watched the people, crossing the road and scurrying along.

When he got off it was growing dark. He walked from Bastille to Belleville, and on to Colonel - Fabien. He entered his apartment and sat down. He'd left a razor blade on the coffee table, and he stared at it in quiet loathing. It was making him look like a fool.

Washing his face in the sink he started crying, the low and useless bulb a witness to his tears. He saw himself as a creature less than nothing, his weakness without end. He hit at his face with a dirty towel.

He climbed into bed and then climbed out again. He stood there clenching his fists. It was freezing, he was just wearing his T-shirt, and he tensed up his body to inflict some more pain.

He spat on the floor and cried again. He didn't even have Karen now. Of course she'd left him forever, of course there was no way back. He punched his stomach, his chest. To even go to that audition was a mistake. He threw the blanket from the bed around him. He went out to the coffee table, and used the razor blade to make lines.

Johnny got up early. He'd been going to the cinema for a week, checking the guide and travelling through town. Hable con Ella, Scarlet Diva, La Haine, City of God. Every film made him want to see another.

This morning, on the southside at Balard, they were showing Once Upon A Time In America. The full uncut four-hours. He finished his coffee and left.

When he arrived, he paid for his ticket and entered. The theatre was very small, twelve rows of red seats, and he slipped in mid-aisle near the back.

When it started, with a phone endlessly ringing, he noticed there were only two other people present. They were both closer to the front than he was, a man and a woman, not together. On the screen a soft breast was exposed.

There was a break after two hours, and he stood outside with the others, smoking amidst small talk. It was a funny moment he thought, the three of them in the middle of the day, sharing smoke and conversation in a quiet part of the city. The day was cloudy and still, a slow, gentle day with a chill to it.

The next two hours passed quickly, spent in the company of gangsters and deceit. De Niro and James Woods had their differences. Johnny scratched a shaving cut around where the jugular vein was, or at least where he'd always thought it was located. He thought maybe his anatomy was shaky.

He let the credits roll before leaving, the amount of people involved in film-making unreal. He read the names of hundreds whose remit he couldn't fathom. They scrolled past, and he sat for a while after the screen went black, and left.

Karen wanted to call him. The first week of December was drawing to a close, dragging the year along with it. The streets were slick treacheries, her skin frozen and wet. It was like they'd made a pact to further her misery.

She spoke to Claire on her lunchbreak, looking for reassurance or guidance or a lie. They discussed it and their coffee grew cold. Karen drew little rings on the table with her finger, making them bigger, smaller, on each lap.

Claire was teasing out ways of prompting Michel to call her, but Karen wasn't interested in that. It was going to have to take the course it took. They ordered more coffee, and Claire changed the subject.

"I'm not sure how long I'm going to stay here," she said. "This job, this city."

Karen was surprised to hear her say it.

Claire had seemed settled, longterm, but maybe something had happened, or she'd simply had enough. Of offices, of Paris. Karen asked why, what is it, but Claire fell silent.

She was quiet too as they returned to work. Karen heard familiar sounds of children and motorbikes. They took the same turn where before there had been a protest, but today there was nothing. The breeze brushed her hair.

Back in the office Karen felt Claire slip away from her. Karen walked to her own desk and sat down. She knew Claire was across the room, settling back again also, taking off her coat. There was chatter and the buzzing of machines.

168

"The more you understand, the more you can accept, and the more you can accept, the calmer you'll be. And the calmer you are, the better you are for yourself, and for the world."
Frank watched her eyes move toward the floor.

She sat still looking down, and he touched her knee.
"I agree with you," he whispered.
She smiled and met his eyes, and leaned over to kiss his cheek.
He rubbed her knee through her jeans.


They were in Aria's place, and Frank had earlier met Laura. An hour later she'd left, and they were alone. His apprehension was unfounded – Laura was watchful, but discreetly. There was no Inquisition, Spanish or otherwise. Aria breathed deeply and Frank kissed her, holding her lip between his lips and stroking her neck. A bin was slammed outside and made them jump.

Aria stood up and boiled the kettle. Frank watched her lean to find a spoon. She was leaving in a week, to spend Christmas with her family, and he was in love with her, and wondering what he'd do. Two weeks away from her sounded like an eternity.

They drank tea on a darkening Saturday, happy to do nothing and then take the metro to the cinema. It was a few hours yet before they had to go.
"So what is this book going to be about?" asked Aria.
"You'llhave to let me read it."
"I'm not sure yet, I'm kind of still making notes. I think I just want to start and see what happens, discover if I can do this, and if it feels like something right. I'd love to write about Sevilla and Berlin."
"I want to see those places. I really want to see what they mean to you. I've been to LA and San Francisco, and once we went up to Canada, but Berlin. I read about it on my flight over here."
"You did? What did it say?"
"Oh you know. It sounded incredible. Full of artists and incredible things."
He smiled and said "yeah, that's what it was."

They finished their tea and she made more. He helped her turn on lights and pull down blinds. She went to get ready, and he looked out the window at the moon. What bastards had taken pictures of this angel he thought. Fury rose and then subsided. It didn't matter, it was gone. He stood in the apartment amidst her kettle and her cups, the softness of her environment.

When she was ready they left. He took her hand in the darkness, and they walked to Goncourt. Teenagers loitered outside kebab shops, knives swished within, and Frank bought metro tickets in the station, a tingling behind his nose. The train juddered momentarily, and Aria fell against his chest. He was delighted and relieved when he caught her.

Laura closed the door, leaving Aria and Frank by themselves. She had no destination in mind. She strolled to Belleville and bought a sandwich in a bakery, watching the woman make it with a delicacy of touch. Yeah, alright she thought, he seemed nice.

This was the first person she'd met from Ireland. He was gentle but not without energy, capable of anger perhaps. That's the way it seemed to her anyhow. She put the sandwich in her bag to save for later.

Her old flat-mate Marie called when she was back on Boulevard de la Villette, a bad line making Laura strain to hear. Marie wanted her to come down, spend some time if she could. It sounded like a nice idea.

On the metro to Alesia, Laura watched a small boy scream blue murder at his mother. He was holding on to a bottle intended for his younger brother, his face red and bloated, his eyes upset and fierce. He was far too old for bottles and he knew it.

His mother wrestled it from him, determined and drained, and the baby snatched it. The stops rolled by, Vavin and Raspail, and finally Alesia. It was a two minute walk to Marie's apartment and two flights of stairs.

Marie let her in with her eye discoloured, a red and sinister mark upon her face. Laura did a double take and Marie stared at her. They went to the couch and Marie began weeping, Laura hesitating, and then putting her arms around her, confused.

Marie sobbed on her shoulder. It took Laura fifteen minutes to make her stop, and another ten to coax the explanation. It was Martin, but he was sorry.

Martin was an English guy who worked in an English pub in the 4th. A sleazy chain for expats with bitter and darts. He was some kind of boss, 27 years old, and had spent the last six years in France. Laura remembered him from when she'd lived with Marie.

There was a knock on the door and Marie froze. Laura didn't know what she was into here. She'd been pushed into this world, and now she was cowering on a sofa with a beaten and frightened girl.

"Marie!" came an English voice. "Ouvre la porte!"

The girls stayed perfectly still. Laura didn't know for how long. It grew dark, and after they heard him leave they didn't move. "He doesn't have a key," said Marie eventually. "He left it here by mistake."

In the tension and adrenalin of the moment, Laura remembered thinking it was strange to hear Marie use English. Then she thought it was strange to even notice this. Her mind wasn't processing properly, she was aware of that. She brushed Marie's hair hypnotically, the girl prone and alert and her small fists clenched. Marie asked her to stay and what could she say.

Djinn squashed the fly in annoyance. It buzzed for a further five seconds, and died. He picked it up and studied it on his fingertip, two legs still twitching.

He scraped it off and flicked it out the window.

The groundward rush separated it into parts. Some school children scampered by below, multicoloured bags with lunch boxes rattling within.

It was hard to kill time on the days he wasn't working. Walking the streets was an option but it brought no relief. He stretched his aching back muscles.

Light was getting caught in the open window pane, making colours like a rainbow. He watched a purple and blue blob dance. The pain had moved from his upper back to his lower, snaking down and twisting inside, and he did more stretches until something clicked.

There was a knock on the apartment door. He stood still for a moment and went to it. A small man of about fifty waited in the hallway, eagerly introducing himself as from the electricity company. They were doing door-to-door checks, some safety procedure.

Djinn let him in reluctantly, and waited impatiently for him to leave. He was gone in less than two minutes. The silence returned to the room, the man's energy banished by the draft. Djinn closed the window and killed the refraction.

Then he himself left, feeling there was nothing to do but walk. The neighbourhood was now disturbingly familiar. It came to him that without realising, he had mapped out walks here also, and unconsciously took different routes that he varied day by day. There were even some sights he looked forward to.

This morning he crossed over to Paris, hovering on the bridge for a time to observe the Boulevard Peripherique. The sign said the traffic was Fluid.

He went up rue Didot and crossed over rue d'Alesia. There was a little playground with some children.

They were very small – too small for school on a Monday, and one of them hugged another and resumed play. He almost smiled but remembered these people were animals.

So he came once again to the tower, drawing him like a magnet. He looked up and thought through the plan. Yes it was going to happen, no sentiment would intrude. Burning flame would carry him to Allah. A dog ran across the road causing consternation, and he felt perhaps this was a small presentiment of the chaos he would create. The world would be turned upside down and would not spin right again.

Aria packed her bag economically. It was only two weeks, and she had clothes and cds at home, so she removed a few items and put the bag on her back to test the weight. It was light enough to carry on the metro.

She was nervous about leaving Laura, after what had happened last weekend. They had arranged that Marie would take Aria's bed, Marie's old one, during the time Aria was away. Still, maybe the guy would come looking for her.

Aria didn't know if she should ask Frank to check in on them. If Frank would like it, or Laura would. She thought he could just call once in a while or text Laura, but she hadn't asked him yet, and might not bother. She threw her bag in the corner and stood up.

It was going to be great to see her family. Ten months was like forever, and she couldn't wait to see her sister in the doorway. Her mother was sure to make a fuss. She hadn't made it home for Thanksgiving, so this would be a double event - turkey, cranberry, the lot. She had presents for everyone from Paris.

She put on music by Lhasa de Sela. She sensed into her body as she swayed. The voice and the rhythm were intoxicating, and Aria felt the floor, through her feet and her legs and her chest.

She felt there was definitely a Christmas feeling in the air. When she walked in the streets there was a magic, a tingling anticipation of warmth and relief. The promise of nursery shelter.

She checked the flight time just to be sure. Re-calculated the right time to leave for it. She remembered that guy who used to curse them from outside, and for some reason he didn't come around now. She hoped he would never come back.

The clock on the wall had long ago stopped working. Aria never tried to fix it, because the ticking she could do without. It interfered with the rhythm of music. She went over to it, the hands still, and took it down and shelved it away.

If Laura liked it there she could replace it. Then Laura returned and Aria said this to her, and Marie appeared through the door. She had a bag and a sheepish expression.

175

They ate dinner together, Marie shy, but the girls chatting to ease her. She was painfully conscious of her face. She had developed a way of letting her hair hang over it, but this required her neck to bend forward, and made her awkwardness even more apparent. She was gentle like a kitten or a child.

Aria watched her discreetly, feeling tears in her eyes as she noticed the tightness and fidgeting. It was searing to see such symptoms in another. Marie extended and re-clenched her fingers, her eyes looking up and down, seeking invisibility. Aria took her hand and held it tight.

Marie stared at her, startled and unsure. They'd never met before in their lives. Aria squeezed her fingers. For an instant the light flickered, then came back on stronger than before. Marie started crying. Laura looked shocked, but Aria was not, smiling to see the shaking in the limbs. Her hand grew warmer around Marie's.

Marie cried for a long time. She sat in her chair, shaking and sobbing and biting at her lip. Aria just wanted to hug her.

Johnny was cooling on his film fetish, having exhausted the Pariscope of material. The problem was the films never changed. He was sitting on his bed. He divided the coke into wraps, and placed the little balls into a drawer. He reached lazily for the guitar. He strummed a chord and it sounded dead.

The other day Michel had asked about women.
"If you give friendly compliments, you'll get friends," Johnny had told him, "and if you praise them like they're goddesses, you'll get sex." Michel had rubbed his chin and thought it over.

Johnny pulled out the drawer and counted how many wraps there were, and then slid it shut. He leaned out the window and spat onto the street, watching the saliva trajectory, and the impact.

He went back inside to get some water. He opened the drawer and counted the wraps again. There were eleven. Eleven fucking wraps he thought, no more no less, and no need to count them again.

The day was threatening activity, a foreboding unknowable something promising drama of some kind. He felt it in his bones. He stretched his arms and yawned.


That night he went out and picked up Claire. Some English girl who spoke good French. Worked in an office and wanted out. Of the job and of the city. He listened to her hard luck story and she brought him home.

She had an elusive quality he'd seen plenty of, a passive kind of taking it. It was empowering and the opposite at once. For him and for her and for them. He wanted to be gone when he was sated, but she held him coldly, with strength. They lay there and their breath intermingled.

His nerve began failing him. She was staring into his eyes. He clicked his tongue but she was unfazed, and it seemed like an excavation she was conducting for his soul. Not born of warmth but of stoicism. He looked back angrily, undressed and with many tables turned. This girl was a mistake.

**177**

Eventually she slept and he didn't. He wanted to leave but could not. She wasn't holding him, he was physically free, but he kept looking at her. She was right without saying a word. He got up with much effort, staring at her as he dressed, and was back on the street.

# BERLIN
July 2001

The band took to the stage. They tuned their guitars, and launched into a bloodcurdling rendition of an Irish folk song. The assembled Germans were aghast.

Frank, Dev, The Behanser, and Pd sweated for the nation. They could see the bar manager regretting giving them a call. Nevertheless, they hit a rousing chorus, The Behanser falling over in the heat and his drugged-up state. Frank knew his sense of timing wouldn't be missed.

Dev bashed the bodhran and Frank strummed unperturbed. Pd hit a high note. The swirl of music, and the crowd, and a head full of E and grass, took Frank outside himself, a guitar strumming, worriless thing. The Behanser got back up and started playing.

When the song finished they slumped and drank. Four more pints would arrive when these were gone. Some places happily doled out drink to them, others needed prodding and suggestion. Frank saw a woman across the room uncross her legs.

The crowd were getting into it now. Pd sang a version of Danny Boy a cappella, roaming about the pub trailing the mic. He disappeared midway through the climax.

On the U-Bahn down to Oranienburger Tor, Frank felt nervous. He snapped out of it when The Behanser gave him a drink. They went into a bombed out department store, a victim of the war and before that the Kristalnacht. Artists and others gathered here. There was a dwarf breathing fire, and a strange dog that was constantly stoned. It chased its swishing tail and drooled saliva.

The Behanser went looking for a dealer. The others could see him crashing about, disappearing behind pillars and reappearing, and then he was back. He sat down and they prepared his captures. Tired after the day. Some girls hovered about to see if they'd share with them.

Frank recognised a dealer he'd seen occasionally, not in this group now loitering, just going past. A little blond German pixie. He held her with his eyes but she ignored him, and then Pd was saying 'that'll floor an elephant,' and handing him a cone. He breathed deeply.

Dev started playing his bodhran like a bongo, patting out a rhythm with his fingertips. Frank lay back using his guitar case for a pillow, every single star up there a galaxy unknown. Every single person and blade of grass. An Australian voice said something unintelligible, hundreds of bodies around, tripping, pissed. On some nights there was trouble and the sting smell of mace.

"Are we gonna get some food," said Dev, "some fucking sustenance." A Hungarian girl sat down beside Frank. She asked his name and then called him Frank Sinatra. *I get no kick from champagne*, he sang in her ear.

The girl suddenly started screaming, and moved her body away from Frank's arm and stumbled into the night. Frank turned his attention to the stoner dog.

It ran over to him unsteadily, a crazed look in its eyes. Pd rubbed at its paw fur. The Behanser came back from the kebab shop, handing out doners and eating a currywurst. Dev started complaining that his had no sauce.


At seven am they crossed the road to a bar called *Obst und Gemuse*. They sat outside with the sun rising, beers in front of them and guitars alongside. Frank went to the toilet and there was graffiti above the bowl.

To be is to do" – Sartre

To do is to be" – Camus

Do be do be do" – Sinatra

He pissed and shook his head and went back outside.

"Possession is not the key to feeling," Dev was saying.

"You can feel bad with a hundred fucking cars."

The Behanser eyed him sceptically, smoking. An unkindness of ravens pecked at something hidden across the street. Pd threw a banana skin and they scattered.

They left soon after, paying the bill and heading for the U-Bahn. They clattered back towards Neukolln, in a four-seat booth each.

**181**

Dev rolled a joint, absorbed in the act of construction. Frank thought of the sun climbing through the world. Each stop picked up commuters bound for work, business suits and builders, the builders with beer in their hands. The steady chatter made Frank want to sleep.

Back in the apartment on Bohmische Strasse, they collapsed amidst bottles and ashtrays, on couches they'd found on the street. An enormous grand piano sat in the corner. Dev picked out a few notes on it, a Bluthner from the 19th century. Pd put his hand down his trousers.

The Behanser stood up and announced he was making soup. They heard the woman who lived above leave with her dogs. The animals scampered down the stairs outside, the owner following with leads tingling in her hands. The leads hit together and made a kind of music.

Frank dozed till the soup was ready, knowing he could sleep for a few hours, and then it was back out to play. On the Ku-damm, in Prenzlauerberg, anywhere. He remembered he needed to buy new strings for his guitar.

Aria and Laura were at the beach, finished with school for the summer, and with only one year left to go. They stretched in the sunshine, the sand soft and delicate, the sky clear and blue.
"When I go to Paris I'll live there till I die."
Aria laughed at Laura's certainty. She curled her toes in the sand and worked out the exam stress, no more need for study before the fall semester began. It was fun to imagine the summer lasting forever.

They applied more sun cream and turned over. The music they were playing was Surfer Girl. Days and weeks could be spent this way, on the sand and by the water, with The Beach Boys on the stereo and the evenings cool and free. Aria noticed some older guy observing them.

He drifted off when she sat up, but when Laura went swimming he approached again. He was handsome, unusually tall. He said she'd make a great model. He said he was a talent scout on this beach and he might have found the one. She could always come along and see if she liked it. She wasn't an idiot she scoffed, and he produced his ID and card. Straight up modelling he promised.

By evening Aria had still kept the secret. Hadn't mentioned the guy at all on the bus ride home. In her room she looked at the card again, saying his number aloud and laughing at the idea.

She stared straight ahead, imagining the life of a model. The guy had said she was the prettiest, sexiest thing. No one had spoken like this before, not the boys she had kissed or her mother. To be sexy was a new thing to be.

They got the U-7 at Neukolln, Karl Marx Strasse bustling and full. At Berliner Strasse, they changed for the U-9 to the Ku-damm. The Mexicans were already playing the red restaurant on the right.

The Mexicans were their competition, two guitars and a violin. Their bellies forced the guitars to be played at chest level. The strings on these instruments were older than the street they were serenading, and flapped about tunelessly as the chords were plucked.

Frank lit a cigarette and watched them. They were sweating in the German summer heat. The Berlin sewer smell rose up violently, making diners cough and Dev complain.

They'd wait half an hour before playing here. After one performance it needed time for the clientele to change. They moved across the road and set up at another restaurant, effortlessly stealing The Mexicans next port of call.

The place was half-empty, and Frank tuned up.
The Behanser wandered off during the first song, leaving him alone to play guitar. Dev sat in front with his bodhran, and Pd slapped his thigh while he sang.

Frank felt light in his head from the sun's rays. He could play the chords to these songs without even thinking. *So Long Marianne, Chelsea Hotel, Lime Tree Arbour.* They played them in cafes, beer gardens, and bars.

The Mexicans in turn leapfrogged them, and the two groups continued around the Ku-damm in this manner, overtaking one another, pausing, and doing so again. Frank's group stopped for beer on several occasions.

Stretching on the terrace of a restaurant they had just hit, they laughed when The Mexicans huffed up and started playing. Frank smiled at finally catching their act. They performed for the customers impassively, staring ahead like they were dead or waiting for a bus. The Behanser let a belly laugh but it didn't ruffle them.

As evening descended, they waited for Dev to drain his glass and got the tram to Prenzlauerberg. There was a square surrounded by restaurants, called Kollwitzplatz.

Here they shared sangria with an English busker named Jason, who told stories of Anderlecht, Paris, and Sevilla. He was maybe forty, with a scraggly ponytail and booming voice. He welcomed the company, and gave a sense of being utterly alone.

Then they started. Touring the restaurants, blasting out the same set. It was difficult sometimes to imbue it with any effort. But they all knew, it was this or working, singing or the building sites, and so they sang, happily. Dev sat on the ground like a beggar or a Buddha.

In a bar at four in the morning they met Martin. An Irishman in an Irish bar in Neukolln. He was thirty-five, from Belfast, and played piano in five star Berlin hotels. The Behanser and Frank invited him back to the flat. He sat at the Bluthner grand, playing Mozart. He launched into Beethoven's Fifth to make them laugh. "You boys are wicked," said Martin. "You're brand new."

Dev tripped over a flashing lamp stolen from a construction site, reaching in vain for something. He stretched out from his seat, then stood up leaning forward. He tripped on the lamp as he lunged at a shadow on the wall.

"Sit down you moron," said Frank.

"There's a fucking shadow on the wall like the ghost of a girl." They all looked, thick smoke obscuring everything, cigarette papers and butts littering the floor. There was no girl determinable.

A carton of sangria had spilled that night or previously, soaking the threadbare carpet, the smell mixing with the smoke. Dev dropped a roach in a can of Kuppers. Frank spied a pack of painkillers on the table and ate the six that remained in it. They combined with the smoke and the drink and made his body numb. He saw The Behanser stand up, but slowly, like underwater. Martin laughed, sounding as though from somewhere else.

"Play fucking piano," mumbled Pd. "I'll sing something Irish if somebody plays."

Martin hit A minor and followed with F. As soon as he moved to G they knew what was coming.

*True you ride the finest horse, I've ever seen,*
*Standing sixteen one or two, with eyes wild and green.*
The Behanser took a block of hash from his anorak.

   As dawn broke they played charades, miming the titles of
films that never existed. Pd took an hour and then gave up
"What the fuck was that?" shouted Dev. "What fuckin' film were
you doing?"
"If you can't guess it, you'll never know."
They sparred back and forth for a while, each claiming the
other's turns were inventions.
The pointless exchange was finally ended with whiskey.

Karen closed her eyes and tried to sleep. She could hear her mother in the next room, not settling down yet, opening drawers and presses. The spirit of her one year dead husband might never let her rest.

From the street outside someone bleeped a car alarm. Karen heard whoever it was trudging up a driveway. A porch door opened, then a hall door, and then both closed again. She guessed it was Jackie or Bill, one of the neighbours working late.

This summer night she had decided to go to bed early. It was a way of taking stock of her life and of feeling like a child. Lying on her back with the top window open, she listened to laughter and traffic, the occasional intermittent sounds of the American night. Oak Park in Chicago Illinois in the house she was born.

Bill or Jackie came back out, and called to someone, and she knew it was Bill. She picked up strains of conversation about the Bears and how they sucked. Beer cans were popped in the warmth of the soft July evening, the men standing on the pavement, probably longing to raise the hood of the car and check the sparks and stuff worked. Karen lay in bed and was awoken to memory.

She thought of her father – how quick he'd be out to join them, ignoring the calls of her mother and barrelling down the stairs. He'd mosey on over and say My God and it's a wonderful evening.

She turned on her side and tried to think of something else. Her mother closed a drawer and then opened it again or a different one.

Karen sat up. She crossed her legs yoga-like, cupping her hands and letting her thumbs lightly touch.

Bill's companion said loudly, "I reckon I'd a caught that."

She breathed deeply to the count of ten, the air filling her lungs and expanding her abdomen. It was easier to think less when the rate of her breathing was slowed.

A motorcycle roared past, swallowing Bill's conversation, and leaving a silence after it was gone. She wondered had the two men been startled by it.

Momentarily they resumed talking again, but it was only to say goodnight. Karen lay back down and drifted into sleep.

Johnny and Lorena carved a melody. She was a Spanish girl who came to him sometimes, and played guitar with him on the piazza. Their guitars wove in and out of each other and intermingled.

Her lines were clean and fluid, Andalucía tinged creations complimenting his, drawing out their sweetness. When he sang she underpinned with fills and flourishes. He leaned back and clicked through his teeth, his tongue flicking out as he hissed to complete a rhythm. Lorena murmured something meant for no one but herself.

Her hair was pulled back tight, clamped in a ponytail. Her eyes danced about and her legs jumped. She'd told him once smiling that calm was not in her vocabulary.

The sun shone on the Pompidou glass, and across the far side from Johnny and Lorena, an African wearing a loincloth was folding himself through a tennis racquet. His audience whooped and cheered when he emerged. He bowed and made some reference to his skinniness - they could see him indicating his bone structure, and drawing a laugh. He climbed onto a tiny bicycle and pedalled around.

Johnny abandoned playing. She continued, forming chords high up the freeboard, creating a high and beautiful delicacy, as she changed with little hammer-ons and runs. Her nails flicked the strings with her thin right hand.

He watched her, rolling two cigarettes absently. When they were ready he placed one on her knee. The body artist folded himself into a crab shape, and scuttled across the smooth tiles at speed. Little children and their mothers observed agog.

Lorena told him of a dream she'd been having, where all the people in the world somehow knew each other. They didn't know that they knew, but a chain existed connecting everyone alive, built on physical contact, mental interplay, and the lightning rush of desire.

"Out of sex and guilt I have filled an ocean," she whispered. "All my dreams of an alternative, perfect life." She used the Spanish for *ocean* and *alternative*, and French for the rest.

He found she often left Castilian endings on similar words. She smoked the cigarette he'd earlier made for her.

A dead bird came hurtling out of the sky. It fell directly in front of them, the violent impact creating a mess. Lorena flinched and stared at it, the beak and feathers mixing with blood and tissue. The internal organs and claws had become inseparable and blurred, a pulpy mass of outside and in. Johnny found himself wondering had it died before landing.

They got up and left it there. They walked to the Seine, descended to the quai, and sat along the bank with the water below them. Lorena was visibly shaken, shivering.

The tourist cruisers rolled past - the sun on the water, the tourists up on deck. Johnny saw a girl wave and returned it lazily. He didn't mind seeing that bird die, not the way Lorena did. It wasn't a tragic event to him, just an act. She curled into herself and clenched her fists, and he was going to put an arm around her but didn't. The spray from the engine of a boat found them on the shore.

Karen balanced the toast on her hand while buttering it. Her mother entered the kitchen and said good morning, an open window ushering in the chirping of birds. Karen listened to their singing carefully, six little arias blending to make a bigger whole.

She finished and stood up, and washed her plate. French grammar and syntax were in her brain. This morning she'd learnt the future for *I will* and *I'm going to*. She had homework to do for tomorrow's class, sentences to construct and read out. She worked with the aid of a dictaphone.

In the garden she sat with her walkman. She drank some iced water and ran her fingers through the grass. It was so strange to know she was leaving, every phone call to Janey an oddity in itself. She'd hang up and remember she wasn't kidding.

Her mother came out and sat beside her. Karen took off her headphones having heard her over the sound. They talked of the flowers in the garden, her mother saying the sunflowers were as high as the fence. A lawnmower from a yard in the vicinity hummed.

Her mother had picked up a summer cold and coughed occasionally, excusing herself each time. She voiced her concerns over Paris. The lawnmower stopped, giving an initial eerie quietness, the kind that arrives when people are unconsciously talking very loud, and then the reason for it evaporates. They realised they were shouting, and laughed. Karen heard her mother scratching her face and exhaling.

"I really do wish you'd reconsider. You don't know that city, and at least here I know how you are. I worry for you, and I'm not sure how much you appreciate that."

"I do Mom," said Karen. "But I have to do this for myself." There was a pause and her mother continued.

"I don't think it will be good for you. I mean going to *Europe* alone. You've never done anything like this honey. And your father never trusted those French."

191

Karen laughed, a laughter flecked with sorrow, and told her mother to stop. She was going and this was ridiculous. "It's still a few months away," she said. "Are we going to have this conversation every day?" Her mother was silent, batted away until the next time, which could be tomorrow, the next day, or this afternoon. Her persistence was the key to her personality.

Karen went inside and into the bathroom. She brushed her teeth and combed her hair. She knew her mother was worried, and sometimes this worried her too. She sighed and reached for the dental floss.

"Have you had your breakfast yet honey?"

Her mother was shouting from the garden.

"Yes," droned Karen to herself. She felt hemmed in and cramped by this scrutiny, and it strengthened her resolve to leave. She slammed the bathroom window in frustration.

Monica was her name. She was watching an unruly musical display, and he went over afterwards and sat down. Performing gave him a strange confidence.

She was from Bologna she told him, over here studying.

"I like the way the songs all opened out," she said.

He agreed, and wasn't sure exactly what she meant. When he said his name was Frank it made her laugh. She called him Frankie for the evening, in the pub and on the bus and in her room. That night they made slow love and he went home.

The lads were awake in Bohmische Strasse, drawing upside down crosses on the wall. Pd was laughing hysterically. He'd been presented with a Black Forest Gateau earlier by a neighbour, and had eaten it all in front of the others. The plate and fork and some napkins were strewn about.

Frank rolled a joint and the buzzer shocked him. Minutes later Martin bounded in.

"Jesus Christ boys, I'm after spendin' all me money on two Russians. I'm all worn out and I think I need a drink."

He sat down, sweating. The tale that followed left everyone mute. Two twenty-five year old blondes had made the Belfast pianist a true believer, with the aid of ropes and feathers and their own God-given secrets and curves. Pd went to the toilet.

When he returned, the smoke had thickened. He fought his way through it and sat down. Frank strummed a melody on his guitar, and squinted around at the bizarre crosses on the walls. Dev poured whiskey on the floor and lit a fire. Blue flame danced for an instant, and then went out.

"With the lights off that'd be brilliant," said Frank.

And it was, flickering and writhing, shadows jumping and alive, smoke seeming thicker than natural. All of them were transfixed in the raging glow.

An hour later a helicopter flew overhead, and in their state they were sure it was coming for them. Frank covered his face with a towel and ran to the balcony to investigate. The chopper was circling menacingly, and he watched it in fear.

It was growing light now, the blue-dawn reality that was their lives. A time when things cemented and got lost when they slept again. Frank stared up at the helicopter, its red body and black wings, the whirling rotors like the charge of some coming apocalypse. He fell asleep on a chair with the towel on his head.

"Get up!" someone shouted. "Get up! There's money to be makin' on the Ku-damm."
Frank couldn't see for a second, and then remembered the towel was blocking his view.
He removed it, shivering in the air, his bones aching and cold. It was probably one or two but it could have been anytime.

Martin was gone, and The Behanser was striding about with a cup of soup in his hand, marshalling the troops for another day's slog. From the bedroom Frank heard Pd groan.
"What the fuck," said Dev, stepping onto the balcony and stretching. His hair was knotted and his face creased. He yawned and spat down below, dredging up phlegm.

They milled around the kitchen, banging into each other and picking at food. They grabbed the guitars and left.

The Mexicans were nowhere to be seen, so they figured they were probably down the far end. They had noticed how occasionally one of them disappeared and was replaced by a lookalike. The same belly, the same moustache, the same instrument. Another compadre allergic to the factory floor.

Dev sat on the ground and fondled his bodhran. Frank could hardly be bothered playing today. He formed chords distractedly, allowing the others to bear the brunt.

Pd slapped his thigh, keeping a rhythm entirely separate to that of the song. The fact no one could hear Dev rendered this moot. The music was greeted with hostility and appreciation in equal measure, and when Pd went round with the boot the collection was average. "Thank you, but no," someone said. "Your music has not pleased me."

After hitting the majority of the restaurants, they packed up and moved towards the tram. The short journey to Prenzlauerberg took them past Hackescher Markt and Rosa-Luxemburg-Platz. .

Jason was on the square, drinking sangria and talking to himself. "Alright boys," he said when he saw them approach. They sat with him and smoked, and it became obvious to them all they weren't going to play that night. They went to a shop and bought beer and jumbo skins.

It grew dark and the night was beautiful. Frank lay back and closed his eyes, his head spinning. He breathed deeply, and thought of hope.

Jason sang a song, an ancient blues from the cotton field. The way he howled and shook he was Johnson or McTell. He convulsed back and forth, his head and body jerking, the strings besieged but holding strong. He spat on the ground and his ponytail worked loose and came free.

*Oh woman what have you gone done to me?*
*Oh woman what have you gone done to me?*
*Well you took my lovin' and then you cut me free.*

The stars hung above, and the sound rose up to meet them. Speech wasn't necessary, and drink was in plentiful supply.

Aria brushed her hair in the mirror. The sun came through the window and onto her desk. She didn't know why, but she always brushed her teeth in the bathroom and her hair in her room. It was her routine, and it stayed because she liked it. The card with the guy's number had been stored in a drawer.

Staring at her own eyes in the mirror, one of her giddy spells came over her - a fuzziness, a rush. She jumped up, the feeling frightening but familiar, her breath spasmodic and short. This frightened her further. She ran to the door and then stopped, thinking frantically as to what had caused it this time. It was like she'd had a sudden recollection of something, now lost.

She went downstairs. Her mother was at work and Anna was at summer camp. She sat on a chair in the back garden, the air bringing relief. Her body was shaking slightly, and she wondered again what had brought it on this time. It was an unsettling stillness followed by suddenly remembering to breathe.

The shock she got began to go down slowly. Voices from the neighbourhood were soothing, carried lightly by the wind. As a child her mother would protect her after these episodes, wrapping her in her arms and stroking her hair. She stroked her own hair now to replicate the feeling.

There was a prickly sensation on her skin. Around her stomach and chest, it felt like tiny scurrying ants. Her legs were heavy and dead. She didn't like this, the thought and touch of it, and jumped up again, scared.

These episodes came and went. Her mother called them her giddy spells. She had had them as long as she could remember. Aria sat down again, stroking her hair and thinking of something else. It was easier to do this when her mother was in the house.

She went for a walk. The street took her away from the introspection of inside. She walked and felt much happier.

A dog ran along the road with a squeaky toy in its mouth – a black and white dog and a red toy. Whenever he swallowed the jaw movement made the thing sound, and Aria laughed, trembling, all fuzzy but in a different way now. He disappeared around a corner and was gone.

When she got back to the house everyone was home. She'd timed it so it would be so. She came around the back way and entered the kitchen, her mother at the sink and Anna drawing in a book.

"A cat is what I want for Christmas," she said.

Aria and her mother laughed.

"Christmas is not for a long time honey. Tell Aria what you got to do at camp."

What Anna got to do at camp was make Batman out of cardboard, a wild mutant creation with pink painted legs and only one eye. His left arm was raised like he was waving.

"And the teacher said that mine was very good."

They all sat down to dinner. Fresh salad was slipped onto Anna's plate, in such a way that she forgot this was unusual. She ate it, oblivious to her aversion, and Aria and her mother smiled but didn't let on. Aria couldn't recall her nerves from earlier.

Johnny smelt *crepes* wafting over. There were tourists in the sunshine with food and drink in their hands. It was packed on the *piazza,* hardly room to swing a dead guitar.

A portrait artist had ensnared an American girl on his stool, and was painting her and flirting with her while she laughed and messed with her hair. Her friends were all standing around with ice cream and Coke cans.

Johnny watched the scene easily. The girls legs were long and tanned. He stood up and rubbed his eyeballs. He had no intention of moving in the deadness of the heat.

He played a song and briefly attracted attention. Not from the girls but from a hobo scouring a bin. The man paused for an instant, training himself on the sound and then resuming searching. He talked in a fast hiss to no one and unearthed some bread.

Johnny took a call from Michel, a nervous new client recently arrived from Bordeaux. He'd met him through Lorena. Lorena was returning to Sevilla in a fortnight, feeling an urge to be back in her hometown, temporary wanderlust sated. Paris is too stressful, she said to him, it's too much.

A man offering shoulder massage set up a complicated chair to Johnny's left, a dentist-like apparatus with a hole for breathing through. The plan was to entice customers to lie on their stomach with their face through this hole, and the man would ease away their aches and pains with his muscle rub.

The first customer pronounced the service excellent. He was an Indian portrait artist, a regular on the square, and he lay down like a dead man, relaxing into the experience and emerging revitalised. Johnny was envious, but couldn't bring himself to do it.

Instead he went to the supermarket, picking up crisps, bread, and cheap champagne. The pop of the bottle was like the start of a party that never was. He chugged it down and broke off some bread, using the champagne to ease the dry food down. The flavour of the crisps was not what he wanted and he dumped them.

Back on the *piazza* the masseur was gone, and a guy making paintings from oil had taken his place. This was real, car engine oil, and the odd black creations were spread out on the pavement for punters. Everyone looked, but nobody reached for their cash.

The guy was churning off the pictures like an assembly line. One would get finished and he'd start another, his face covered by a mask. The paintings were all much the same, the painter's jeans soaked in oil.

They rang at the door but were turned away. The Madame peered out from the gloom, shook her head, and the slit they could see her through closed. They were standing on the street at 4am.

Frank, Dev, and Martin were desire's captives. This part of town had red neon and mirrored facades. It held promises of sin and swollen lipstick.

They turned down a side street and were beckoned by a doorman. "Good deal," he said. "Beautiful girls." The man was Turkish and overweight, in his fifties with a lime-green shirt. Martin spoke in German to better negotiate.

Inside, an ancient piano propped up a wall bedecked with sparkles. Girls sat at the bar, an older woman served. Through a half-open curtain they saw an obese German with two girls astride him, his tie on the floor beside a bucket of champagne. The speed they'd taken earlier was wearing off.

"Whiskey," said Frank. "You know, fucking whiskey."

"Ja, ja, I know."

The barwoman busied herself mechanically, pouring Wild Turkey and, before they could stop her, adding Coke. Frank curled his lip and refused to go near it.

"What," she snapped. "You say whiskey I do fucking whiskey. Drink, drink."

Frank gave her the evil eye but took it nonetheless.

A girl approached each of them, and before Frank knew it, he was on a stool with her hand on his crotch. The other hookers watched them, bored.

"So tell me your name, and your country." She rubbed him and he rubbed back, the whiskey foul.

"Ah, Irish. I love the Irish music." From the corner of his eye he saw Martin stroke a dark girl's hip.

"Yeah, Irish, and where are you from?"

"Potsdam," she said. "Are you going to buy me drink?"

Frank said he had no money. She looked at him coldly and he swore he really had none.

"You won't buy me drink?"

"No."

She turned away from him. She was still beside him but it was like he wasn't there. Her eyes were dead and when he spoke to her it echoed into nothing. The other girls did the same, Martin and Dev declining also, and the bar was now a frozen den of hostility.

"What the fuck are you doing?" said Martin. "We were promised a show."

The barwoman stared at them bitterly. Dev looked at Frank and they were almost going to leave.

"We were promised a show," repeated Martin, louder.

A wizened little man appeared from somewhere.

"Make show!" he ordered. "Make show!" He clapped his hands and grabbed roughly at the black girl, and she stood up and walked towards a pole. "Make show!" he said again, and music began.

She swayed, comatose, her body forming shapes but her eyes not there at all. Frank drank more Coke and nearly wretched. He pushed it away and watched her naked gyrations. A mirrorball hung above, purple and blue light catching as it spun. Frank noticed how her shoes were so worn, battered silver sandals holding hard-skinned feet. She caressed herself like a zombie.

"Lets go," said Dev. "Fuck this."

The old man hovered over them, imploring them to stay for more booze.

They sat in the Schwartze Café with cream coffee. Martin was talking about artists who made paintings from shit. It was an hour since the brothel, fully light when they came out, the sun climbing. The streets populated by cleaners and staggering drunks.

"Yeah, yeah, seriously boys. Their whole manifesto is art from bodily fluids. Shit, blood, semen. They work in warehouses and squats, and this stuff sells big time in markets."

Frank began to feel queasy, unsure.

Dev spilled sugar over himself. He cursed, but the waiter was laughing.

"Machts nichts," he called over, uncaring.

They got the U-Bahn back towards home. Martin got off at Gneisenau Strasse. On their balcony Dev and Frank composed poems of that night.

"The fuckin' eyes in the place," said Dev. "They hadn't seen light in twenty years."

Frank drew a picture of the girls and threw it down to the courtyard.

They had a bottle of what the label called 'Breakfast Cider.' It was a strange, fizzy, non-alcoholic carbonated applejuice, and they guzzled the whole thing with pastries.

"I'd love a fucking sausage roll, or some chicken," said Dev, dropping crumbs.

It was ten o'clock. A bright, hot mid-morning, the snores of Pd and The Behanser carrying out through the bedroom window, droning softly in time.

Frank whacked his knee with the empty plastic bottle, and a bird squawked and took off from a roof. The sound reverberated around hitting concrete and windows.

"You should always seek out the quiet parts of a new place," said Dev.

"The quiet parts can make even an old place new." They drank the rest of the juice in silence.

They went shopping on Michigan Avenue. In a coffeehouse on the corner of Monroe, Karen again felt frustration from her mother ordering for her. She knew she meant no harm, but was stressed nonetheless.

"I'm not gonna have that Mom," she said. "I haven't decided yet."

"Oh, I'm sorry honey. It's just that normally you - "

"I know Mom, I know."

It was busy around them. A lunch time rush in the centre of downtown, and Karen felt hurried and observed. Her mother's company made her painfully aware of herself.

*

In a snack bar in San Jose Aria finished her burger. She drank Sprite and watched the diners come and go. She surprised herself when the straw reached the end and she started slurping. All of the ice in the world was nestled in the cup.

*

In a café in the 6th, the newly arrived Michel Rigaudeau from Bordeaux fiddled with his napkin. His hair needed cutting and his shoes begged for repair, but this was only because he liked them, and resisted buying new ones. The waitress watched him curiously.

An old man called Boulier sat at the far end, an infrequent visitor, with his hat and his cane. He occasionally came here having strolled in the park with the pigeons.

*

Karen and her mother left the shop. On the street they ran into Dorothy, who was complaining about Archie and the ways he drove her mad.

"I'll leave him one day you know, permanently."

They said goodbye and went to get the El, pushing through throngs with the office workers freed.

"Hold that fucking door!" cried someone.

The train rattled westward, moving through Cicero and Austin, heading home. The heat was stifling, bodies everywhere and the humidity high. Karen held her stick and felt sweat on her palm.

"It's just incredible what crowds there are. I knew we should have tried to beat the rush. I said that honey, didn't I, that it would be like this."

Karen agreed, yes, you said it, wanting to be back in the garden, or anywhere else. She heard a man selling cookies like a preacher from the slums.

"Oh yes, and then the LORD told me something. He said Leroy, for that's the name I was born with, he said LEROY, you go out and sell those cookies, for ME, and for the CHILDREN. And I am IMPLORIN' all you good folks here today, to BUY some of these here fine cookies, and help us all spread a little love. Every little cent's another miracle."

Karen closed her ears to him, concentrating on her breath. Her stomach rose and fell. This trip would end she said to herself, this day, this month and whatever was coming. She would go to Paris and be happy, and start something new.

There was a gig to be done before leaving. It was in a beer garden by the river, with a wooden stage and tokens for drinks. Each of them got three tokens.

Frank's strings were so worn it was difficult tuning them. He wound the pegs in the sunshine, knowing his time in this city was nearly through. By nightfall he'd be on a bus out of town.

Patrons drank and ate schnitzels and currywurst. Children, old people, Africans with dreads, expats. In the corner by a pool table Turkish girls showed off their thongs.

"Remember," said The Behanser, "we've got to do three fucking hours here."

Pd had disappeared to smoke and use the phone.

"I was just saying there," said The Behanser on his return, "take your time on this one. If anyone wants to try anything it's all part of the song."

Dev scraped his nails along his bodhran saying it was good for the skin. A child wandered over to investigate and ran back to her mother.

"And a one, two, a one, two, three, four –
Oh come over to the window my little darling…

They started as they always did, So Long Marianne by Leonard Cohen. Frank felt he must have done it more times than Cohen himself by now. He watched his hands make the chords, not thinking.

One tune followed another, with extended instrumental parts, and more beer breaks than the tokens warranted. At one point a Rasta with his own drum joined them on stage.

"I hope he doesn't think he's getting in on the cut," said The Behanser.

"Well if he does we'll just break it to him gently," said Pd.

They took a rest at four, stretching out on wooden benches and rolling grass. Frank had broken a string but was unconcerned. The crowd was shifting before them, people drifting in and out and some staying for a while. It was a no-pressure gig – they just had to keep the music coming and the money was theirs.

"This next song is for all the ladies," said Pd, not realising his fly was undone. The Turkish girls in the thongs ignored them like flies. Unperturbed, they stuck with it, sweat on their brows and lightness in their hearts. The song for the ladies turned out to be a folk song about death.

The owner appeared to one side, her arms folded, but a smile on her face. Some people in the audience were clapping and so was her son. Frank sensed another string about to go, and then it cracked loose and whipped out. The Behanser beefed up his strum to compensate if he could.

In the end, they got paid and went drinking. There was a bar boat docked on the far side of the bank. They walked across, the river sparkling.
"So here's to you Frank," said Dev. "Sure we hardly knew ya."
The others raised their glasses to toast his last day. Frank found it a sad and hectic experience, the knowledge this part of his life was over. Everything was so fast, and blurring, and gone.

How long he had been in Berlin he couldn't say. It was a fantasy camp, a dream. He felt a tear in his eye and finished his beer. Berlin when day broke was the reason God gave him breath. The sun in the sky and the ache in his soul. The hope that his hope would never desert him in conflict.

The water was rippling gently down below them. He was noticing details now, the sound of traffic in the distance. A bee landed on the table, paused, and flew off again.
"It's at nine o'clock the bus, yeah?" said The Behanser.
"Sure you've plenty of time so."
They played cards and remembered stories, the day of departure bringing a softness no other could match.

It was evening, the moon visible but the sky still bright.
They were camped around Zoo Station at the terminal.
A beggar with a McDonalds cup drifted about, requesting money in a whispered, alien tongue. His hair was matted and congealed like a wet dog's.

The hum of bus engines and the smell of petrol was familiar. Drivers stood around talking, passengers smoked last cigarettes. One or two kids loitered to watch bags loaded on.

"There's loads of fuckin' nuns around," said The Behanser.

"I wonder are you going to be travelling with them."

"You can give them a good seeing to," said Pd, smiling.

Frank showed his ticket to the driver. It was last call, most people already in their seats now. The lads all shook his hand and folded their arms.

"We need smokes," said Dev to The Behanser.

A tyre squealed in the traffic. Frank had Monica's U-Bahn map in his shirt. With one final nod he turned to the door, and looked up at the driver, his hand on the wheel. It was a long old journey he thought, from pleasure and strangeness to the unknown.

He grinned. He was safe in the knowledge he could always come back. The city would still be there, forever. Frank gripped the handle, and got on the bus.

# TE QUIERO

It was February 6th 2004. Aria was twenty years old. Frank, Laura, and Marie watched her blow out the candles, one staying lit until she blew it again. Aria kissed her friends and picked up the knife.

"Moi, je ne veux pas beaucoup," said Marie.

"Too late," said Aria, laughing.

Frank rotated his ankle, and watched her cut the cake.

"I think we should sit down for this," said Laura. Perhaps she'd noticed Frank's pain. They sat around the table.

"Make a wish when you cut it as well."

"But I already made one when I blew it."

"Doesn't matter. Go again."

Dancing crumbs hit the plates, rolling and clinging to forks and teeth. They drank champagne, bubbles on their tongue, laughter. Aria looked so happy.

"So where are we going tonight?" said Laura. Aria said she didn't know, and it didn't matter.

Frank glanced out the window, catching movement in the flat opposite, a girl hanging out a pillowcase and singing a song.

Marie had been living here for a few months now. When Aria returned, it was decided she stood stay. The three of them had gone out to buy a mattress. She slept below Laura's loft, in the other room, a curtain giving privacy.

When they did go out it was to Montmartre. The girls danced, and Frank rolled his ankle and watched. He thought Aria was so beautiful in the neon light. She came to him, and they kissed in the darkness. Her body fell against him, a little drunk. He held her tight, her familiar smell. She laughed tucked into his neck, and he felt her breath.

"If your leg is sore we can go."

"No, it's not. I can't feel it."

They danced slowly, swaying as one. Her hair tickled his cheek. Some guy tried to muscle in but Frank pushed him off.

"I love you," he said quietly, and she didn't respond.
"I love you," he said again.
"I love you too," she said.

Johnny stood by the window, a cigarette in his hand. It was cold outside, mid-February grimness. He pulled off the butt and dropped the remains to its fate. Someone had been working late last night, new graffiti all over the wall opposite.

The confines of his room were sufficient for today. He was sure he wouldn't leave unless it was necessary. He smoked another cigarette, returning to the window. The kebab shop up the street was emitting steam. He watched for a moment, the white billows curling upward, and then a small Turk came out flapping a towel. He cursed and waved it, coughing, and laughter could be heard from inside. Johnny coughed, and turned towards something else.

The clack of high heels had caught his attention. A working girl prowled up the street, incongruous in daylight – fishnets, heavy make-up, high boots. Her dark skin was worn and made her look older. She picked at her lip as she passed the kebab shop door. The inevitable whistles and catcalls ensued. She seemed more warrior-like than sexual, and he thought she possessed a marauding fierceness. Frizzy hair like Medusa.

Johnny's phone buzzing made him lose her. He checked it, looked back out, and she was gone. He stayed where he was, looking up in that direction at nothing at all. There was a red garage door he'd never noticed before.

He stared at it. It was weird – so obvious and blatant now. He spat down below and wiped his jaw stubble. He ate some bread and pretended it tasted better. He drank water and felt breadcrumbs sticking in his throat. He worked his neck muscles and swallowed.

Melissa had not been around lately. He hoped for her sake it was nothing more than her mood. She was prone to lose consciousness occasionally, to collapse in a heap from not eating. He thought of her for a second, on someone's floor, and felt cold.

In the evening he went back to the window. It was dusk, twilight, people returning from jobs and physical toil. Factory hands, labourers, bakery assistants, and the partners of drunks.

Johnny saw a little child scamper ahead of her mother, an enormous African woman in traditional dress. The girl hid in a doorway and pounced, but the mother was unflappable, deadpan and burdened with bags. *Ha, ha,* said the girl, and received a clip on the ear.

The moon rose and emptied the darkening street. Some brothers stood around, punching their chests.

Johnny smoked, and nodded his head when they waved to him. It wasn't a wave, just a raising of the hand by one. The sense of community could be strong in the quartier, everyone seeming to know where everyone lived. It was hard for him to escape the idea his history was known.

"*Ca va?*" came a call to his right.

He turned his head, and coming down the street was Michel. Johnny spat, and went to look for the key.

Karen put down the phone and shivered. The typical office noise was around her, appliances, sales chatter. But now there was no Claire and lunch was long.

The phone rang again, and as she fielded some routine query she thought of Michel. It was months before, pre-Christmas, since she'd heard from him, and anything he might do now would be too little too late. Time had simply parted them and she wasn't sure how.

She took a stroll after work, just walking in the office vicinity before going home. A friend, and a lover, vanished in the past. She had compartmentalised her life – Claire her workfriend, Michel her boyfriend. Now these two were gone, and Janey she rarely saw.

The wind was biting, howling in and out of the spaces between offices and through the car parks. She tightened her scarf and lowered her chin.

Rounding a corner a gust hit her, whistling through her body and making her pause. She lowered her head still further and squeezed shut her eyes.

At home that night she listened to the radio. A jazz station playing John Coltrane. She wondered what it was like to make such notes from your breath.

The drums were frenzied but clinical, the bass a slithering eel. It was cacophonous or perfect and she didn't know which. She tied her hair into a ponytail, sitting on her bed fully clothed. A strand of hair behind her ear slipped out and hung down.

The DJ came on and said that track was from *A Love Supreme*. Then she went on about the suffering in Coltrane's life. Poverty, spiritual anguish, shooting smack to relieve toothache and other physical pain. He was an unusual man she said, who could pick his nose right in the middle of a concert.

Karen stood up and stretched. She went to the kitchen and leaned out the window into the night. It was too cold to do this for long, the air sharp in her nose and mouth. The occasional sounds were harsh on her tingling ears.

Back in the bedroom she lay down and slept with her clothes on. She awoke in the early morning shivering and climbed under the sheets. Traffic sounds were already audible, the beeping of horns like John Coltrane. *Parp, parp, honk* went the cars, and all that was missing was the scattershot fills of the snare.

Djinn flung the frozen lasagnes into the compartment and slammed the door. His fingers were numb and wet from melting ice. He cursed to himself and rubbed his hands on his jacket. A thread caught his nail and the feeling was nearly more than he could take.

The plan had been delayed. It should have happened by now. He had encountered certain difficulties. The attempt to procure vital material had been met with suspicion by hardware store employees, and he'd been forced to retreat. Now he was buying small quantities at irregular intervals.

He surmised that records must be kept. When, where, how often, designated products were bought. It made sense, but he'd failed to think of it. It was better to travel throughout town, obtaining small, insignificant amounts, with no discernable schedule or regular sum. It was time consuming, but the alternative was possible failure.

He walked back to the storeroom and sat down for a moment. The light in here was softer than the harsh neon strips. He closed his eyes and listened to his breath in his body. The simplicity of breathing was what he was looking for now.

He stood up and returned to work. The freezers were taken care of and now it was on to the drinks. Endless fizzy bottles of sugar being consumed and needing to be replenished. He watched a fat man fill up his trolley in disgust.

Someone pushed past him and grabbed two bottles of Coke. He stood still, enraged by this brusqueness, and then slowly turned around and headed for the store. A dropped tin of peas meant he also needed the brush.

The peas had travelled far and wide, an unwelcome fact he discovered upon his return. They were under other produce and hiding in cracks. He swept as best he could, finding it amazing how much dust could accrue. He'd only cleaned the floor that morning.

His hand was sore against the ageing brush. The wood was coarse and splintering, jagged needles pushing his skin. He knew the best solution was a towel wrapping.

"Pardon," said someone. "Le vin, s'il vous plait?" He pointed in the right direction and the customer shuffled along the aisle.

After work he walked the streets. A light picked up his shadow and then it was lost, only to re-emerge in the beam of another. A prostitute said *Bonsoir* and he put his head down.

He came around a corner and walked into some skinheads. They pushed against him on purpose and his balance was gone. He crashed sideways on top of a bin, feeling its corner smack his hip as the stench hit his nose. *Fucking Muslim* they called him, *Fucking Al-Qu'ida*.

He lay on the ground. They circled above momentarily, spat, and went on. He listened until their footsteps were faint and straightened his clothes.

Dreadful shame made him shake for an instant. He looked about wildly, to see if someone had seen. There were lights on in apartments, but no figures in the windows. He clenched his fists and felt tight pain in his jaw.

The garbage men were trawling about, jumping on and off their trucks and seizing the waste. Djinn watched silently, feeling calmer now. He thought that job might actually have been better than the supermarket. Out in the air, clinging to a truck, learning about the city and not dealing with the French. Just throwing all the stuff into the back and climbing on again.

He looked up at the sky and tasted blood on his lip. He hadn't been hurt, but was insulted they'd managed to draw blood. The taste was bitter copper, returning from whence it came.

Michel climbed off the whore, her eyes like a fish. She was Nigerian and clearly repulsed by him. He hoisted up his trousers, his belt clicking off his zip. The walk back out to the street was the part he was dreading.

It was still bright, half-four in the afternoon, a weak sun on rue Saint Denis and the techno music from clothes shops. He scurried around a corner and nearly hit someone. "Quoi," said the boy, in rap regalia, open mouthed.

Michel excused himself, walking on. He felt he really needed a toilet quick. That old nervous bowel-loosening, catching him short on rue des Lombards. He ducked into a tourist restaurant.

He emerged and was right beside Beaubourg, but didn't want to see Johnny. His stomach was dancing, churning, and his heart beat fast. He had a sudden urge to retch, but nothing surfaced. He just did it there on the street, the muscle action sore.

Soon afterwards he did get sick, under Pont des Arts, urine in the air. A homeless man's dog sniffed against him and disappeared. Michel read some chalk on the wall saying Defense de pisser.

He leaned on a wood beam, his body shaking and his eyes unclear. The smell of the place caught in his throat like acid. His cocaine use had increased dramatically. Karen was gone, and she'd been his reason to be.

He stumbled down along the quai side. His pulse was jumping in his wrist like a jackhammer surge. It was odd to be outside in such physical discomfort, the feelings in his body more appropriate to staying in bed. For the tiniest second he desperately wanted his mother.

He sat on the ground. It was dark - heavy clouds, the river beginning to churn violently, like before a storm.

It had risen, he was sure of that, and he watched and listened to the current roll. The river was menacing in the darkness, no tourist boats, nothing. The coldness of the ground made him want to get up but he did not.

"I hate Michel," he said. "I hate fucking Michel."
A roar of traffic from the Right Bank Expressway drowned him out.

He stayed for some time, reluctantly standing eventually. He took the metro home and fell into bed. It was true he thought that he wasn't handling things well, true what Johnny had said. He needed someone in his life or his life didn't happen.

Laura picked up her discman and put it in her coat. She was in l'Observatoire, just behind the Jardin du Luxembourg and south of the Sorbonne. She had a break between lectures It was a narrow strip of greenery with kissing couples and joggers.

The sun was shining, the warmest day in quite a while. It was early March. Laura had been listening to Aimee Mann, thinking of the days when herself and Aria sunbathed at home. Three years she thought, is both a long time and an instant.

Four children walked by in a line, with their minder a little behind them. They held each other's coats with tiny hands. The first one stopped, bending to examine some gravel, and halting the entire train. The other three waited placidly and then moved on.

Laura sat thinking. She remembered a quote from an old Japanese man on tv. *Watch a football match like you're watching a tree in the garden. Just look, and be contented by the looking.* It had been on a programme to do with stresses of the modern age.

She took in the scenery around her, the trees, grass, walkways and people. For a second she had the strongest sense they were the same. No difference existed between a woman and a flower. Every single eyelash and every blade of grass were at one. Then it was gone, and she was smiling.

She stood up and prepared to return to college. She gathered her jacket and bag and the packaging from her lunch. It wasn't a difficult afternoon, the emphasis firmly on exams now, and she knew despite her tiredness it would easily pass. The traffic on St. Michel grew louder as she approached.

She crossed the road and entered through the gates. The smells and bustle of the corridor made her feel young. Finding the correct room, she sat down near the back and rooted for a note pad. All of her colleagues, or most of them, shuffled about.

Later she studied in the library. It was easier to get work done here. Two guys nearby giggled over a magazine. Laura tried to concentrate on her assignment, but it was hard, and she had to ask them to stop. They stared at her like she was a shrew.

The book-lined shelves granted more peace occasionally than the study area. She wandered among them, only half-heartedly searching for books. The wood smelled to her of lonely academia. Reading about blood she thought, is not the same as the swish of the knife.

That night she lay in bed and dreamed of a boy who might understand her. He'd have no interest in hairgel or strategies of cool. She turned over unconsciously, folding into herself when she heard a sound. A magnified shard of reality infringed on her sleep.

Frank was writing about his time in Sevilla – of meeting Lise and Sjal, and drinking with Dev. He found it an odd but beautiful experience to put things down. In a way, dredging up these memories for a book was a method of releasing them, a benign and gentle freeing of thoughts in his head. He would scrutinise them closely on paper and then find they were gone.

Writing let him taste and smell in ways he'd forgotten. Sevilla was sensually rebirthed to be fully let go. He remembered small moments – light on glass, wine, laughter. His body seemed to rewind also, and his ankle grew sore.

He stopped for a moment. He rotated the muscle and cartilage till it loosened and felt warm. Slowly he read over what he'd done. He didn't know if it was any good or not, and he didn't really care.

He walked around the room with his pen in his mouth. Some paper fluttered towards the window and he hurried to retrieve it. It was a page where he and Lise played pool in some bar.

He heard a helicopter in the distance and then silence returned. He wanted to write about Aria and wondered if he could. Might he jinx the sweetness of his reality? He thought it better to finish the Sevilla section before contemplating this.

He wrote down a conversation between Lise and Sjal. An English conversation, because they didn't want the others excluded. It was something to do with awareness when they entered a room.

Lise had said she unconsciously registered who was where upon entering a room. She thought Frank did it also but Mette did not. He transcribed these sentences as best he could, knowing exactness was impossible and approximation would do.

He boiled water for mint tea, taking a break and leaning out the window. March, and the weather was suggesting it was May.

This was two years in a row – unexpected sunshine in February and March. When he thought of his discomfort a year ago he was amazed at so much change.

He began writing again. Once, Sjal and Pernilla had taken him to the coastal village of Torrox, and he remembered clear blue water and banana splits. They stayed in a house owned by Sjal's parents, with a rat in the kitchen.

He jotted down descriptions. He didn't know any of these people now. Probably he could meet them again and still not know them, or maybe not. Perhaps he'd get re-acquainted with them afresh. The sun hit his desk and dust was visible. Aria had told him that dust made her think of a plane.

He swished his hand through the air. Dust particles scurried and re-aligned. He was going to write something about humans being like dust, but deemed it pretentious. Humans are more like moths he thought, attracted to what can hurt.

He didn't know how long these pieces he was writing were going to be. He thought he would write about Berlin and leave Chicago alone. Reminiscences of Berlin and Sevilla would be perfect.

Aria sent a text and he read it three times. *I'm making dinner tonight. Come over x*. A bird on a balcony opposite broke into song.

Aria bought chicken, peppers, and tomato puree to make a sauce. She had rice already, but needed milk. Curry powder and bread she nearly forgot, but then remembered, and went back down through the aisles and had to queue again. A little kid stole a stranger's juice at the checkout.

Dinner was going to be for four people. Herself and three others in her life, all of whom she loved. Laura was making salad, Marie was getting wine. She could send a text to Frank and that would be that.

The walk home took her past scaffolding and bars. It was only five minutes, but she heard six different tongues. Builders, drinkers, loiterers on the street - the multicultural city, functioning as one.

She pushed in the front door, the wood expanding occasionally, and needing to be forced. There was music coming from inside, and then she saw Laura and Marie, washing cutlery and singing.

"Well, I got it. A little girl stole some guy's juice just after he paid for it."

She put down her bags and stretched, feeling light in her head.

Movement to her right made her turn. A cat charged across the floorboards and jumped onto the sill. All three girls saw it simultaneously, the black feline streamline so alien in the flat. It stopped to lick its paws, and looked at Aria full on. Did it feel it was safe at the window and no longer need run?

They stared as it went about its business, cleaning, stretching, and eyeing the roof. Its whiskers twitched as it crinkled up its nose. Then it sneezed, sneezed again, and Aria laughed.

"It's the curry powder. The smell must be crazy to a cat."

The cat seemed to confirm this by sneezing again. Then it spilled itself out the window and was gone. Marie went to see if it was still down there, but there was nothing, just the bins and the courtyard and the steps. Aria unpacked the shopping and prepared to cook.

Johnny was back at Beaubourg. The sun was shining, lending everything a faintly promising light. He took out a cigarette and smoked between songs.

"Hey Mister," said someone. "Hey Mister. Why aren't ya playin' somethin'?" He looked up to see a small red-haired boy of eight or nine squinting at him quizzically. He was chewing gum, and the flavouring was red on his tongue.

"I'm tired," said Johnny. "Where is your mother or father?"

"None o' your business," said the boy, and ran off.

Buskers gathered over the far side, two young bucks in plaid shirts. A singer and a guitarist, the singer with a tambourine. They launched into some Eagle's tune. Johnny picked at his nails freeing dirt from the underside.

*"Come on baby, don't say maybe…"*

"…I've got to know if your sweet love is going to save me!" shouted Johnny. A few people looked, and he stood up, beaming.

He hadn't seen Michel in a while. A month or so, infinity by Michel standards. People pushed gently along across the square, a hit parade of flip-flops and cameras. Paris in the springtime, and the burden of the romantic myth.

Johnny contented himself with watching the throng and listening to The Eagles covers. All the classics got an airing, one after another in the sun. *Tequila Sunrise, Hotel California.*

Pigeons scampered about in search of bread. The pigeons, the buskers, the tourists, the drunks. Beaubourg he thought, was the world in a manageable size.

The sound of a saxophone was audible and then not. Johnny swivelled his head, trying to make out where it was coming from. The breeze and the chatter were revealing and then concealing the notes, lending it an extra-plaintive air. Then he sourced it, a guy in a beret hidden under the library façade.

Now he could see the guy the music was constant. His senses were working in tandem, sight aiding sound. All he had to do was keep looking, ignoring the occasional obstructions of tourist heads.

The Eagles cover band had stopped. One of those weird moments happened, where suddenly the square cleared. It was Johnny and the jazz artist, frozen, and then there were people everywhere again, posing for pictures and feasting on *crepes*. The guy kept on playing, squeezing juice through the tube.

Johnny lit up a cigarette, letting all the other sounds encroach on him again – children, a siren. A pigeon landed on his shoe and then flapped away in fright, its internal radar askew. "Welcome to the Hotel California," said Johnny. "Such a lovely place, such a lovely face." Then he sang it, keeping his voice gentle and low.

Karen walked by the river. The first Saturday in April, reasonably warm, and she knew it was between ten and eleven in the morning. Her stick scuffed off a tin can and she redirected herself slightly.

She heard a tourist cruiser approaching, a voice announcing in English and French the proximity of the *Quartier Latin*. The boat was coming from Pont Neuf, heading east.

She walked on, letting the morning pass. Janey had called the day before, and they were going to meet later. Karen smelled fast food, and heard teenage voices. Some happy group by the bank, sugared up and flirting.

A xylophone melody floated across the water. She didn't have a clue what it was. It was caught in the air and chiming, this strange little sequence of notes.

She strained to hear more. It was too late, it was gone. There was just the flow of the water, and an alarm going off somewhere. Soon these banks would be filled with tourists. Already she had noticed an increase. Still, on a day like today it was possible to walk, the congestion not so total that her liberty was gone. A dog ran by, the sound of his lead hitting the cobles.

An hour later she was at l'Hotel de Ville. She had crossed over Ile de la Cite, taking in the feeling of a now gorgeous late French morning. Notre Dame and the American voices. The place next to l'Hotel was crowded also, but she sat at the rue de Rivoli end, letting the sun hit her skin.

She thought of where she might walk. She didn't want to go home, but it was necessary to plan a route. She could take rue du Temple, swing a left onto rue Reaumur, and then another left at rue du Louvre would bring her back towards the river. She heard a child demand ice cream and be denied the request.

The sun on her face brought back memories of Chicago. With her mother, in the garden. The sensation of her neighbourhood, the remaining presence of her father. A shadow scanned across the sun, the coolness interrupting her.

She got up and took the walk she had planned. Through the Marais and back around by the Louvre. At Pont des Arts she sat on the bridge, and heard performers and their audiences.

She had moments where she wondered should she go home. They had increased of late. Little nagging ideas - perhaps it would be best. Her family, her own people. She could catch a plane, touch down in O'Hare, and be back in her hometown, full of promise. But she was in her hometown now she said to herself, by the water.

Djinn wrote a letter, and then rewrote it. He wanted to send it to a newspaper, to arrive the day after the event, so it had to be precise. It would land in the offices of *Le Monde* when his body was charred. He could not let them think it was a random or meaningless thing.

He had terrible pain in his back, and stretched gingerly, feeling ugly friction and strain. He reached around to rub at the area, massaging as best he could. Then he stretched too far, and the pain nearly made him cry out.

Young people in the hallway surprised him for a second, their voices and laughter passing by his door in a rush. They were running down the stairs into freedom. He breathed and stood completely upright. Awareness of pain was bringing more pain in his shoulders and legs.

Ninety minutes passed with him relatively immobile. It was serious effort to walk to the bathroom and piss. Fortune or the lack of it dictated the agony didn't cease, but instead remained active, feeding off itself, adding to his distress. Finally he managed to lie down on the bed and try to sleep.

When he awoke, the immediate impact of his predicament hit him hard. He couldn't get up. He was sure of it, knew it instantly, and lay there inert, gripped by paralysis. It wasn't even painful anymore, just numb.

Silence and darkness were all around him. He prayed through the silence and darkness and towards Allah. If it was decided he would do this, that he would take revenge for his country and its suffering, he must walk, and function.

He focused all his energy on rising. His muscles shook, but he failed in his attempts to sit. Sweat broke out on his forehead, tiny helpless beads, and the pain from earlier came flooding back from the force. Never in his life had he known such incapacity.

He sat up eventually. He pushed himself into a position that was a crouch or a hunch.

He stared straight ahead into blackness not seeing a thing. It was a struggle to believe, but a struggle he knew he would win.

Laura remembered the day, Aria having called in the early morning. Saturday, and Laura groggy on the phone.

"What, you want to talk now? What's wrong? What's the matter?"

Laura had known there was something the matter for months. This had affected their relationship, made it hard and uneasy and false. Conversations like actors rehearsing lines. Wiping foam from the dishes in their Paris apartment, Laura smiled, and felt sad and alone.

Marie came in. She'd been in the other room, tidying around and re-arranging. She said a room never grew stale if its contents were moved.

"Ca va?"

"Ouais ca va. Tout va bien?"

"Oui – mais je suis fatiguée."

"Moi aussi," said Laura, "moi aussi."

Marie dried the plates and the rest. She stacked them and put them in cupboards. The day was overcast and threatening rain, bringing a heaviness inside as well. The lack of energy in the air was infectious and tough to counter.

Laura smiled at Marie. The way she just came in and helped immediately. It brought back a memory of when it was the two of them here, before Aria arrived. It was a flashback experience to see Marie stacking the plates.

Laura rinsed a cloth and ran it over the table. It caught in a splinter and the noise tingled through her teeth. It was that momentary shiver, a whistling blackboard intake. She rolled her shoulders and carried on with the job.

A crack of sunlight appeared, a laser beam across the wet surface, and then thinned even further and was no more. Music from another apartment took its place. It rushed in, fast heavy metal, startling the two of them by how loud and unexpected it was. The thump of the drums.

"Oh, mon Dieu," said Marie, putting her hands over her ears. Laura closed the window, but was laughing at the same time.

"You don't like that?"

"Quoi?" shouted Marie, not hearing.

There was a commotion down in the courtyard, the same women who complained about the bin usage, now up in arms over noise pollution. Soon the song ceased.

"C'est fini," said Laura, making a finished motion with her arms. Marie took her hands away from her ears. The silence was broken by the clucking tones from below, the women, having dealt with the music, seizing on the opportunity to once again fuss over the bins. The wrong material was always in the wrong compartment.

"Les poubelles encore?" asked Marie.

"Ouais," said Laura. "Naturellement."

Michel knew he was in trouble. He had no money of his own, and the rent contribution from his parents had gone up his nose. And the loss of his girlfriend had allowed all his confidence slip.

This confidence desertion was compounded by his poverty, because no money meant no coke. Cocaine was all he had without the warming sense of comfort brought by Karen. He had used it sparingly back then he thought, more sparingly than recently anyway. He hadn't seen Johnny in he couldn't remember how long.

Six weeks? Possibly. It was the middle of April, and it was raining. He lay in bed and shivered, not sure if he could stop if he tried. The sound of a drill hummed outside.

Under the covers was hot - stifling, clammy. He didn't want to stay, but couldn't surface. The drill pierced into his head, feeling like a rattling in his skull. The sweat on his hands was alarming him.

He was often tempted to ask Johnny for credit. He knew the answer in advance, but dreamed of it anyway. Still, it was more than this imagined refusal that stopped him going. He didn't want to see him, and had felt so for a while.

He propped himself up and looked around the room. His clothes were strewn about in disarray. Jeans entangled in shirts and socks, a jumper draped across a chair. He saw one of his shoes, half wedged behind a cupboard.

He got up and leaned out the window. He held this nagging insistence that Karen would call. It came and went, stronger, weaker, and it wasn't so simple as to fade the more time passed. That morning it had been so real he was tense with anticipation.

A ladybird crawled across the windowsill and onto his hand. It opened its wings, preparing to fly. A rustle of wind kept the wings open, but the creature stayed put, its legs on his hand too small and delicate to be felt. The tiny black wing spots were perfectly round against the red.

It was Sophie who drew ladybirds, his five year old cousin from Bordeaux. She drew endless little pictures of these insects with grass and a sun. On the fridge of her family home, in her bedroom, smiling ladybirds eating or drinking tea.

Michel watched the one on his arm fly off.

His nostrils itched. They were frayed and scratched and sometimes bled. He thought he would rather stay at this window eternally than turn back to the room.

A queasy sensation came over him. He lurched forward and vomited onto the street. He could taste it in his throat as he gagged, the hot harshness of it. His insides stung, and the peace of the aspect was shattered.

Aria stood by the water. The day was monkishly still, death-like, very little traffic on the river or the streets. It was Sunday afternoon, two-thirty. She had the strangest feeling something was imminent.

There were no birds, and they often congregated along the bank. There were no tourist cruisers or pleasure boats. Instead what existed was a foreboding buzz, an energy crackle neither obvious nor sweet. She was aware of heaviness all through the muscles of her legs.

She walked along towards Pont Neuf. The water echoed under the bridge as she approached. The lapping was menacing, a child's nightmare storybook lap. The monstrous stillness was crushing with the urine smell.

She hurried forward. Back out in the air, stopping, she looked across at the Ile de la Cite as it neared the tip. She turned around towards home to get out of this atmosphere.

The flat was empty. The night before Frank had taken her to a gig. She was a little tired, dozy, and fell onto her bed still wearing her shoes. She thought she probably wouldn't sleep, but just lying might be enough.

An unusual sense of impending remained. Her eyelids fluttered involuntarily. Her mind hovered above, watching her curled form, seeking out the plateau between asleep and awake. She gave a start and stretched out her arm.

A tender breeze whistled through the skylight, but it failed to relieve the static of the day. It was a reminder of the absent alternative, a more lively, active world, and turned a spotlight on the choking humidity. Aria placed her hand on her stomach and breathed slow.

Her abdomen rose and fell slower and slower. The more she became aware of it, the fuller her breaths became.

In time she fell asleep with her hand still resting there. A part of her was conscious of the lifting motion in her dreams.
She dreamt of seeing that LA boy enter a clothes shop, and of running after him in vain.
She didn't catch him, and forgot about it after she woke up.

With Laura and Marie she ate dinner. The three of them around the table as a self-contained whole. There was caesar salad in the middle and bread to be torn off. Aria drank a little wine, still tired but content.

Marie was complimenting the cooking. Laura batted away her praise and told her to eat. Aria wanted to speak of her feelings by the river, but they weren't so pressing now. There was more of a lull in her mind, a calming hush.

She tore off more bread. It was fresh, warm, broken easily. The chicken was seasoned, the rice light. Nothing tasted in any way different than it should.

There was an explosion at Montparnasse. Frank heard it from his room, but he didn't know what he'd heard. He was in the middle of writing a sentence, when a deep and terrible boom sound brought him to a halt.

It was mid-Monday morning. April 19th 2004. He sat frozen for a second, the adrenalin rush giving him a fright, and then went to the window. The neighbours began poking out of flats below and opposite, all heads craned in the direction of Montparnasse.

"C'est les terroristes!" cried an old woman. "Les terroristes!" Frank looked across and saw her peering from behind a curtain.

Pretty soon, after a few minutes, a burning smell hit them. It was evil and nasty in the throat, and Frank saw smoke rising in the sky to the north. His view was obscured, but he immediately thought of the tower.

La Tour Montparnasse was never visible from Frank's apartment. He wasn't that high up, and buildings blocked the way. Nevertheless, he knew exactly where it was, and the thick smoke lifting looked to be spot on. He got a phone call from Aria, fear in her voice.

She was at Saint Germain des Pres with Marie, and had seen straight down rue de Rennes to Montparnasse. The tower had collapsed just like the ones in New York. He could hear how terrified she was, a soaring sense of panic making him chill. He wanted to be there or transport her quickly to him.

On his own street now there was pandemonium. The sound of sirens and screams carried through the air. Fire trucks, police, ambulances and the CRS, all careening towards the scene or heading off crowds. Frank told Aria to go home and ring him when she got there.

He didn't know if she would. Immediately afterwards he tried to call her back, but the signal was busy and then died. He kept on trying, wishing they'd never hung up.

Why had he been so stupid? He should have kept her on the line until she was safe. Three, four minutes passed and still no connection, and he cursed how careless he'd been to allow the call end. There was sweat on his forehead and hands, a bad taste in his mouth.

He left the flat. This was pointless, futile he knew, but he wasn't thinking. No sooner had he arrived on the street than a cop pushed him back. "Rentrez!" he shouted. "Rentrez-vous!" Frank tried to explain that he couldn't possibly just go home.

The policeman was distracted by a scream and Frank charged away. He got up onto rue Didot and the scene was unreal. A stampede of people was hurtling towards him, office workers, residents, children dismissed from school and couriers with bikes. Cars and vans were blocked in the roadway, some abandoned, others holding frazzled but impotent men. The police were ordering the evacuation of all vehicles and shops.

He tried Aria again. He couldn't even hear a tone, but the screen said no link. He saw with dismay his battery was running low. The physical mush of bodies was oppressive, everyone hyped-up and wild. Children with their mothers were terrified, chaos all around.

Frank finally made contact. He ducked down rue Morard, and when he heard her voice his panic subsided. She was ok she said, they'd been herded the far side of the river.

Barriers had been put up at Chatelet, and this is where they were, the CRS with bullhorns attempting to manage the mob. Somebody whacked against Frank and he nearly dropped the phone.

"So you're fine?" he shouted in the receiver. "You're really fine?"

"I'm OK," she said. "We're gonna try and get home."

"I'll make it somehow. It might take forever but just ring again when you're there. OK? Promise me." Her voice was drowned out as a police bike screeched to a standstill.

"Rentrez! Rentrez!" This was all they could think of instructing the public. Go home to your houses, get out of the streets. Frank started heading east, away from his apartment.

At Tolbiac things were quieter, and all buses and metros had stopped. He was trying to move fast, before roadblocks were in place. On a couple of occasions he skirted cops angrily chasing him, and the pain in his ankle shot through his leg like a bolt.

He crossed the Seine at Pont de Bercy, after an hour. On the bridge he could forget there had just been an attack. He found progress easier on the other side, taking a wide route towards Republique. He was asked for his address, but simply gave Aria's flat. Within another hour and a half he'd arrived at her door.

The four of them together made the sense of shock less overwhelming. The burden of total confusion could be shared around. Frank realised he'd walked for three hours in a daze, a blurred adrenalin momentum it would be difficult to replicate. He remembered pausing on the bridge, and thought it utterly surreal. Aria played with a small silver ring on her finger.

The body count was increasing, 2,000 people missing or presumed dead. The tv spoke of blood streaking the pavement. Frank's sense of time was horribly askew, and he no longer had any idea of the sequence of events. How long after he'd heard the sound before the madness in the streets. His mind contained a jumble of imagery, flashing sirens and faces locked in fear. He still felt he heard the cries and shouts in his ears.

It seemed like the city had been stolen. The magical swirl of darkness and light spirited away. In its place stood a war zone of barriers and entrapment. The notion of going to a café had been rendered absurd.

Frank watched repeated footage of the tower surroundings. He was already certain these pictures would remain in his head. No one had captured the explosion itself, or at least no one so far discovered. All that could be shown was rubble, corpses, and smoke.

"I can't get through to my family," said Laura. Frank had never seen her vulnerable and fragile before. Sitting in a chair with the phone cord round her wrist, she was like a child.

"It's the system," he said. "It's just it can't cope with so many calls."

He told her to try again in a few minutes, but she didn't, and redialled immediately.

Aria looked out the window at the courtyard. Tvs in other apartments showed the same as hers. She knew now she was lucky to have caught her mother a little earlier, even though news of the bomb hadn't yet filtered through. Aria had had to tell the whole story, explaining she was fine.

The tv speculated on possible perpetrators and motives. It was odd how quickly they jumped to an Arab link. Talk of September 11th, Bin Laden, Afghanistan training camps and Islamic extremists. They didn't have a shred of information or fact. The news anchor reminded viewers of previous terrorist threats in the nineties and before. For a second he seemed to flirt with the notion it could be ETA or the IRA. Then he returned to the Muslims.

Marie asked to turn it off for a little while. Frank wanted to stay watching, but the girls did not. In the silence they heard the newsreader on someone else's set. The muffled voice continued to struggle to make sense of it all.

Frank felt exhausted. Tiredness swooped down over him, and his body slumped in the chair. His eyes closed and his mind went on stand-by, his ears not accepting external stimuli anymore. The last thing he remembered was Laura saying who wants tea.

A week after the event it was still the only news item. The death count had become an official tally that was fluctuating less. 1,410. It was conceivable more bodies would be found, but Karen knew it had stayed at this figure for two days already. She knew also that a letter had been sent to *Le Monde*.

The sensation caused by this discovery was refusing to abate. It had arrived in the paper's offices on Friday 23rd, which made it late according to its postmark, but service had been disrupted. The letter provided the bomber's rationale, and was splayed across the front page. Every other newspaper reprinted it as soon as they were able.

Karen had heard its contents read out so many times. On the tv, the radio. Every day she took five calls from her mother, pleading with her to come home. She wasn't sure why, but the event had seemingly hardened her resolve to stay.

She'd made sure Michel was OK, not thinking, just phoning automatically. This was on the Tuesday, twenty-four hours post-attack. He'd sounded so down, but he hadn't been near the blast. The conversation ended when he launched into a speech about needing her.

"I just wanted to make sure you weren't hurt," she'd murmured, saying goodbye.

It was strange how occasionally she could forget everything, doing the ironing, dusting. For perhaps a five minute period there had been no bomb. Then she'd pause, and it returned. It was such a hard to gather together alien thing.

She had immediately seen it in global terms, speculating. As bad as Chirac was, surely he could avoid the mistakes of Bush. The government noises had been dignified and appropriate thus far, but what they might lead to, who knew. Often, failing to sleep, she pondered various likely and unlikely outcomes.

She hadn't stopped walking, not seeing any reason why she should. From the subdued streets, it was obvious many others did. At normally busy times of the day there was a pronounced hush, striking on a bustling thoroughfare like rue de Rennes.

General uneasiness remained in the city. The buying of goods and services had a mechanical feel. The tone of life in a shop or park was one of abject confusion – the atmosphere of a wake following an unexpected death.

Karen began tuning out of the endless news bulletins. It was clear that nothing was being said. Theories, ideas, no more or less informed than her own. She took sanctuary in her everyday routine, exercising, working, and understanding the event for what it was. It was not the apocalypse. Life was continuing.

On a bus she heard a conversation between two old women. *This is what happens when we let those people live here.* What people she was going to ask, but why bother. She knew such an attitude lives to snatch at reasons to exist.

Chirac said calm was necessary. Raffarin said much the same. The streets of Paris were morgue-like and uncertain, and most people simply stayed in doors. Birds and rodents never had it so good.

Johnny sat, tuning. It was an empty square now. He assumed they were all spooked by that explosion. The sound of the strings echoed off the concrete and glass.

He had only heard about the bomb two days afterwards. He'd been sick, huddled in bed, some ugly spring flu. It wasn't until he'd ventured out on the streets that he'd seen the newspaper headlines. He'd been cocooned away, oblivious to the splash and its ripples.

Perhaps it was this absence that lessened the magnitude. When he finally became aware, it was not so overwhelming, not so strong. Montparnasse was an area he rarely if ever visited.

He strummed a C chord, but the B string was still out. It needed to be flattened by the slightest degree. He played a progression of C, G, Fmaj7.

A piece of paper skitted along the ground. It blew closer, and revealed itself to be nothing. Just a torn off segment from the classified section of a newspaper.

Suitable apartments had been ringed in red by the owner. He stretched out, picked it up, and scanned the page. Various possibilities were circled and ticked.

Johnny let the paper blow on again. It rested for a minute beside him before crawling down the slope. He massaged his forehead with his fingertips, moving down to rub his eyeballs and the bridge of his nose. His cheeks felt coarse.

Lorena had once said melody is human duty. The rhythm in your step and the lilt in your voice are your own. It's impossible to live unmusically she told him, so a choice exists between flowing purity or low atonal drudge. Johnny considered it a fanciful idea, but not an irrelevant one.

Curious noises became audible, like a hacking cough. He listened carefully, this desperate bronchial sound shredding through the air. It rose and fell, stopping and starting, wrenched misery escaping from a stranger's soul. Somebody in the neighbourhood was doubled up getting sick.

Aria pulled up the shutters and unlocked the door. The place had an unusual aura first thing in the morning, unsullied by customers and motion. She flicked on the power, and started warming bagels.

The mirror along the wall was sporting a smudge mark. She must have missed it the day before. The warm bagel smell hit her nose as she rinsed a cloth and eased the smudge to a memory. She ran the cloth over the tables, straightening crooked napkin dispensers.

While the coffee machine shuddered, she wrote on the blackboard and placed it at the door. The guy across the street in the flower shop nodded hello. She heard the coffee percolating and paused in the morning sun, half-inside, half-outside the cafe.

She raised the blinds and the sun crept in. It stretched a quarter of the way across the first table, and she smiled when she thought it would slowly fill more of the room. Its gentle advance would accompany her through the day.

Dust was visible in the air, catching in the rays and dancing about. She was going to swish it with the cloth, but then didn't. Already it was May, and she had been in Paris over a year. Whispers of trauma were almost inaudible in her soul.

She replenished the fillings running low or whose appearance was unsavoury. Red onion, olives. The cookie jar looked a little grimy, clouded, so she emptied the cookies out and gave it a wash.

The sun was now a little further. It was in possession of the first table, and had begun serenading the floor. The brightness was revealing more marks and spots. Aria checked her watch and there was still time before opening. Enough to restack the chairs and mop the floor. Bubbles fizzled in the bucket as the mop plunged, clinging to the tentacles and sploshing down on the tile. She chased them dry with a brush, and re-set the furniture.

She expected the owner in today but didn't know at what time. Because of this it was awkward to invite Frank for lunch.

It had happened before that he'd been halfway through a sandwich when she'd arrived, glaring suspiciously and clicking her tongue. Frank had had to pay, handing over a fistful of coins.

Karen was a customer who'd recently started visiting. A blind girl, American also, from Chicago. Aria found her easy to talk to, wise and with plenty to say. It was impossible not to marvel at her strength.

Aria never said this to her, but couldn't help thinking it. To be so worldly and competent and yet unable to see. She suspected Karen knew she thought this, even from their minimal customer-waitress relationship. Karen's movements were all so flowing and defined.

They had never spoken about the bombing or its aftermath. Karen had been in four times, twice post-explosion.

With the floor dry, the tables clean, the bagels warm and the fillings ready, Aria stood back and looked at the perfect café. In five minutes time it was officially open, but if someone came in now she wouldn't make them wait. A breeze pushed through the door, and ruffled one of the napkins.

Frank put the gathered nail clippings in the bin by the door. His fingertips tingled, and he ran them under warm water. He always kept his nails so short people asked him did he bite them, but he didn't, never had. He looked at his fingers, the right middle finger bearing a scar.

On Pont de Bercy the world had been frozen. Sculpted, hardened, and left hanging for him. A gap in the chaos he had left and the girl he was going to.

He sat down and stared at his manuscript. It was growing – moving and shifting, the relevant and less so pushing for space. Is a person on a page automatically a character he wondered, immediately imbued with this status, and changed. Can writing about something alter it, make it less real? He wasn't equal to these questions.

He wrote a sentence and deleted it. Various alternative constructions began swimming in his brain. He had cleaned his room thoroughly in the morning, getting up early to do it. Now, at the stroke of twelve, he was rooted to the desk.

A glass of water sat beside him. Tiny bubbles floated toward the top, slowly, ponderously. He saw the smudged imprint of his lips in two different spots.

He went to the window and leaned out. One of those sci-fi cleaning vans arrived, scuttling down the road with a hose attached. There was a man attached to the hose, walking along the path spraying the ground, and from Frank's position it looked like the man was leading the van. Walking his green and yellow dog.

The hose writhed and rolled from the vehicle to the man. The water cracked and splashed on the butt-strewn pavement. Frank could still not make out the van's driver, and he tried not to look, lest he shatter the illusion. Pedestrians took refuge on the street to avoid getting soaked.

Frank went back to his desk. He fiddled with an odd piece of string protruding from his wallet, a straggly end where the lining had come loose. He looked at a picture of himself on his ID card.

He rotated his ankle. Muscles were caught, and there was clicking, and pain. He rubbed it slowly, methodically.

The sound of a circular saw skewered the silence. A pinpoint sound, like an opera singer in a bad mood. It darted out, finding Frank in his room.

He tried to describe it accurately. Even if it didn't make the scene it would be useful to do. Take the senses and filter them through the fingers, put down what is heard, what's seen.
He wanted clarity. Precision, lucidity, economy of expression. Words on the page because they had staked a claim to be there.

The wind blew the curtain and it fluttered in the bedroom. He imagined for a second he was in a film, a handsome young actor playing Frank. The camera would leave him to his writing, and move maybe skyward, or fade to black.

Karen smiled at the memory. The sound of a cruiser brought her back to the present. It was early June, she was by the river, but she'd been in Chicago in a daydream, a birthday party long ago. She felt the slightest tickle of spray on her face.

Sunshine, sympathy. Paris was promising gentle delight until August. She'd go home when it grew stifling, although it would be in Chicago too, and then return afresh in September, rested. Already it seemed like the days were rolling as one.

She heard a recorded voice from the tourist cruiser. *The bridge we are passing now, Hemingway once spat off the side.* The spiel was trundled out in English, then in French.

She leaned back, her hands on the cobbled quayside. She knew the exact distance from her outstretched legs to the bank. The sun was warm on her face, but there was still a coolness seeping through underneath. A suction heaviness, tiring and deadening her limbs.

She shifted position. The movement brought warmth, but then the coldness again permeated. She stood up. Another cruiser could be heard approaching from the west, the battleship hum increasing in volume. It was fascinating to her the way the water was ploughed. It was a pushing certainty, the slow movement of the boat fixed on its task.

She felt a one euro coin in her pocket. Something inside her said she'd been keeping this for a reason. She rolled it over between thumb and forefinger, not removing it from her jeans.

She had hunger for a crepe, the butter, the sugar. Lemon juice maybe. She began walking east, along *the quai*. She passed under the urine soaked bridge at Saint Michel, the reeking one with the little steps down and back up again. She sensed the presence of homeless people, and heard a dog.


She eventually found herself wandering in the Jardin des Plantes. The smell, the feel of plants and foliage was everywhere, a thick density of growing, feeding things. She listened to the sound of the gravel as her feet pressed into it.

She walked around, twice having to ask people for her bearings. She did this matter of factly, at ease. She had long ago learned that the manner of asking determined the response, a simple, direct question giving a corresponding reply. It was only if she made a fuss that the other grew flustered.

She came back around by the main quayside entrance. The one she had entered through, the way she would leave. A guard bid her good day as she passed under the gate frame. Without thinking she turned her head and did the same. This is what people should do she thought, in a place they call home.

He stared up at the clock. A gentle sun was hitting the clockface, the white of it gleaming beneath the numerals. Pigeons rested on the roof tiles, gliding towards the ground to scavenge for food. Whenever one found some, a fight would start. The flapping of the wings and the pecking was upsetting, but he didn't know why. It was an ugly spectacle to witness, to be so close to.

Johnny tuned his guitar and gently touched the strings. He had placed the case out before him on the tile. The place de l'Hotel de Ville was busy but peaceful, less frenetic and fast than the piazza Beaubourg. Today, for the first time in his life, he wanted to sing to them.

He started quietly, feeling into things, never having played here before. Rising confidence raised the volume, and it began to feel natural. Soon coins were dancing in the guitar case, fifties, ones, even a five euro note. It seemed to him he was singing clearer than ever before.

His fingers pushed down the strings, new strings he had bought a week before. They were settled now, no longer slipping out of tune. He felt so centred, making chords, changing, the notes he was producing from his body and his guitar tangled up together. He glided one finger down the fret board to harmonise.

A few business types stopped before him. Three men, two women, smart suits and briefcases. The interest of two of the men was the reason they had stopped. The others fidgeted, hoping by a collective leaning motion to move the party on. After a moment it worked, the interested two showing disappointment.

Johnny moved his legs, keeping time. His head rolled, and his shoulders kept tightening and releasing. The sun grew stronger, bathing the square in beautiful light. He closed his eyes and inhaled deeply through his nose.

He felt the buzz of a text message in his pocket. Then another one, or maybe the sender had sent it twice. He looked up at the sky, a plane flying high overhead.

But Johnny wasn't going anywhere. He let himself imagine what it might be like to be on that plane, travelling somewhere, excited. The tingling anticipation of coffee in another land. What was the use? He was where he was, a guitarist on a Parisian tile square.

He stood up and stretched in the sunlight. He massaged his neck, then pushed his shoulders towards his ears. He could hear the clicking of muscles bunched up, feel the strain of freeing what was used to being caught. His body was so hunched he thought, so constantly bent and folded.

He thought he'd stay playing for another hour. He'd recently been toying with the idea of getting a job. Nothing too big or stressful, nothing intolerable, but dealing drugs was no longer where he wanted to be. It was depressing, all those fuckers with their jittery eyes and pale arms.

He started another song. A slow one. His hand changed chords without him needing to think. He strummed and picked, singing loud, but gracefully, not barking it. The birds and pedestrians were sought out by his voice in the air.

Frank and Aria spent the afternoon at Allee des Synges, sitting on a bench, watching the water. Before leaving they wandered down to the Statue of Liberty, and stood staring at the calmness of the Seine. Frank told her it was his favourite view in the city.

They held hands lightly, fingers gently kneading. An easy breeze played and danced with their hair. A tourist cruiser rounded the jutting walkway they stood on, returning towards the Eiffel Tower and the place it would berth. A pretty little girl waved her hand and they both waved back.

Aria pushed a piece of gravel over the jetty's edge and smiled at the plop. She looked down at the dirty, clouded ooze. There was all manner of contaminated rubbish probably buried there, bottles, cans, condoms and long disintegrated bread. The water made a lapping sound against the stone.

Frank was going to look at her but stayed looking at the water. Their hands were barely touching, so lightly it tickled. In another second he thought maybe she would pull away from him. He felt electricity in his fingertips.

The sun shone on their faces, and she squinted. It was Bastille Day, the 14th of July. The evening would bring fireworks, drinking, a celebratory disruption of routine. Austere parts of the city held hostage by noise.

Aria walked over to the statue, and sat underneath. She was half in sunlight and half shaded. Her hair fell across her face and she seemed to Frank a stranger. For a split second he had no idea who she was.

Her left eye was hidden, her lip curling upward. It was an angle, an expression, completely new, transforming and surreal.

He stared and she noticed him, and then she broke the spell and smiled.

He walked to her, sat alongside. He knew she didn't want him to touch her, not in that moment, and that was fine. He scratched the back of his neck where he felt he'd been bitten.

The sun pierced through a cloud, unsettling, stabbing. He felt suddenly afraid, utterly alone. He turned to look at Aria, and she was looking at the ground, her hair falling down, her hands placed neatly on her knees. He became aware of his breathing, and was crushed in deep sorrow.

Would this ever fully go? Could it always return to unnerve him on a whim beyond control? Awareness, negative focusing, impeding the ability to just sit, stand, walk. Perhaps it could only be accepted he thought, his reality when it came.

She threw her arms around him. She just slid over and embraced him, holding him tight. He started crying, and laughing, his body reaching for hers. She caressed his face, sweet water from his eyes on her wrist.

His arms were around her waist, her back, Frank desperately trying to communicate more than he could. To hold, squeeze into life what words couldn't say. In the sunshine, in the summer, at the foot of a statue in Paris in 2004. He wanted some gesture or motion that said nothing but love.

Lightning Source UK Ltd.
Milton Keynes UK
10 November 2010

162656UK00001B/1/P